D0001483

A Little Book

OF

WESTERN VERSE

A Little Book

OF

WESTERN VERSE

BY

EUGENE FIELD

NEW YORK

CHARLES SCRIBNER'S SONS

1904

MANHATTAN PRESS
474 W. BROADWAY
NEW YORK

5615

The Contents of this Little Book.

MARY FIELD FRENCH.

A dying mother gave to you
  Her child a many years ago ;
How in your gracious love he grew,
  You know, dear, patient heart, you know.

The mother's child you fostered then
  Salutes you now and bids you take
These little children of his pen
  And love them for the author's sake.

To you I dedicate this book,
  And, as you read it line by line,
Upon its faults as kindly look
  As you have always looked on mine.

Tardy the offering is and weak ; —
  Yet were I happy if I knew
These children had the power to speak
  My love and gratitude to you.

                              E. F.

*Go, little book ; and if an one would speak thee ill, let him
bethink him that thou art the child of
one who loves thee well.*

A Little Book of Western Verse.

───◆───

CASEY'S TABLE D'HÔTE.

OH, them days on Red Hoss Mountain, when
    the skies wuz fair 'nd blue,
When the money flowed like likker, 'nd the folks
    wuz brave 'nd true!
When the nights wuz crisp 'nd balmy, 'nd the camp
    wuz all astir,
With the joints all throwed wide open 'nd no sheriff
    to demur!
Oh, them times on Red Hoss Mountain in the
    Rockies fur away, —
There 's no sich place nor times like them as I kin
    find to-day!
What though the camp *hez* busted? I seem to see
    it still
A-lyin', like it loved it, on that big 'nd warty hill;

And I feel a sort of yearnin' 'nd a chokin' in my
  throat
When I think of Red Hoss Mountain 'nd of Casey's
  tabble dote !

Wal, yes; it's true I struck it rich, but that don't
  cut a show
When one is old 'nd feeble 'nd it's nigh his time
  to go;
The money that he's got in bonds or carries to
  invest
Don't figger with a codger who has lived a life
  out West;
Us old chaps like to set around, away from folks
  'nd noise,
'Nd think about the sights we seen and things we
  done when boys;
The which is why *I* love to set 'nd think of them
  old days
When all us Western fellers got the Colorado
  craze, —
And *that* is why I love to set around all day 'nd
  gloat
On thoughts of Red Hoss Mountain 'nd of Casey's
  tabble dote.

This Casey wuz an Irishman, — you 'd know it by
    his name

And by the facial features appertainin' to the
    same.

He 'd lived in many places 'nd had done a thousand
    things,

From the noble art of actin' to the work of dealin'
    kings,

But, somehow, had n't caught on; so, driftin' with
    the rest,

He drifted for a fortune to the undeveloped West,

And he come to Red Hoss Mountain when the
    little camp wuz new,

When the money flowed like likker, 'nd the folks
    wuz brave 'nd true;

And, havin' been a stewart on a Mississippi boat,

He opened up a caffy 'nd he run a tabble dote.

The bar wuz long 'nd rangey, with a mirrer on the
    shelf,

'Nd a pistol, so that Casey, when required, could
    help himself;

Down underneath there wuz a row of bottled beer
    'nd wine,

'Nd a kag of Burbun whiskey of the run of '59;

Upon the walls wuz pictures of hosses 'nd of
    girls, —
Not much on dress, perhaps, but strong on records
    'nd on curls!
The which had been identified with Casey in the
    past, —
The hosses 'nd the girls, I mean, — and both wuz
    mighty fast!
But all these fine attractions wuz of precious little
    note
By the side of what wuz offered at Casey's tabble
    dote.

There wuz half-a-dozen tables altogether in the
    place,
And the tax you had to pay upon your vittles wuz a
    case ;
The boardin'-houses in the camp protested 't wuz a
    shame
To patronize a robber, which this Casey wuz the
    same!
They said a case was robbery to tax for ary
    meal;
But Casey tended strictly to his biz, 'nd let 'em
    squeal;

And presently the boardin'-houses all began to bust,
While Casey kept on sawin' wood 'nd layin' in the
dust;
And oncet a trav'lin' editor from Denver City wrote
A piece back to his paper, puffin' Casey's tabble
dote.

A tabble dote is different from orderin' aller cart:
In *one* case you git all there is, in *t'other*, only *part!*
And Casey's tabble dote began in French, — as all
begin, —
And Casey's ended with the same, which is to say,
with " vin ; "
But in between wuz every kind of reptile, bird, 'nd
beast,
The same like you can git in high-toned restauraws
down east;
'Nd windin' up wuz cake or pie, with coffee demy
tass,
Or, sometimes, floatin' Ireland in a soothin' kind of
sass
That left a sort of pleasant ticklin' in a feller's
throat,
'Nd made him hanker after more of Casey's tabble
dote.

The very recollection of them puddin's 'nd them
    pies
Brings a yearnin' to my buzzum 'nd the water to
    my eyes;
'Nd seems like cookin' nowadays aint what it used
    to be
In camp on Red Hoss Mountain in that year of
    '63;
But, maybe, it is better, 'nd, maybe, I'm to
    blame —
I'd like to be a-livin' in the mountains jest the
    same —
I'd like to live that life again when skies wuz fair
    'nd blue,
When things wuz run wide open 'nd men wuz brave
    'nd true;
When brawny arms the flinty ribs of Red Hoss
    Mountain smote
For wherewithal to pay the price of Casey's tabble
    dote.

And you, O cherished brother, a-sleepin' way out
    west,
With Red Hoss Mountain huggin' you close to its
    lovin' breast, —

Oh, do you dream in your last sleep of how we use
    to do,
Of how we worked our little claims together, me 'nd
    you?
Why, when I saw you last a smile wuz restin' on
    your face,
Like you wuz glad to sleep forever in that lonely
    place ;
And so you wuz, 'nd I 'd be, too, if I wuz sleepin'
    so.
But, bein' how a brother's love aint for the world
    to know,
Whenever I 've this heartache 'nd this chokin' in
    my throat,
I lay it all to thinkin' of Casey's tabble dote.

LITTLE BOY BLUE.

THE little toy dog is covered with dust,
    But sturdy and stanch he stands;
And the little toy soldier is red with rust,
    And his musket moulds in his hands.
Time was when the little toy dog was new
    And the soldier was passing fair,
And that was the time when our Little Boy Blue
    Kissed them and put them there.

"Now, don't you go till I come," he said,
    "And don't you make any noise!"
So toddling off to his trundle-bed
    He dreamt of the pretty toys.
And as he was dreaming, an angel song
    Awakened our Little Boy Blue, —
Oh, the years are many, the years are long,
    But the little toy friends are true.

Ay, faithful to Little Boy Blue they stand,
  Each in the same old place,
Awaiting the touch of a little hand,
  The smile of a little face.
And they wonder, as waiting these long years
      through,
  In the dust of that little chair,
What has become of our Little Boy Blue
  Since he kissed them and put them there.

MADGE: YE HOYDEN.

I.

AT Madge, ye hoyden, gossips scofft,
      Ffor that a romping wench was shee —
" Now marke this rede," they bade her oft,
      " Forsooken sholde your folly bee ! "
But Madge, ye hoyden, laught & cried,
      " Oho, oho," in girlish glee,
And noe thing mo replied.

II.

No griffe she had nor knew no care,
      But gayly rompit all daies long,
And, like ye brooke that everywhere
      Goes jinking with a gladsome song,
Shee danct and songe from morn till night, —
      Her gentil harte did know no wrong,
Nor did she none despight.

III.

Sir Tomas from his noblesse halle
  Did trend his path a somer's daye,
And to ye hoyden he did call
  And these ffull evill words did say:
" O wolde you weare a silken gown
  And binde your haire with ribands gay?
Then come with me to town ! "

IV.

But Madge, ye hoyden, shoke her head, —
  " I 'le be no lemman unto thee
For all your golde and gownes," shee said,
  " ffor Robin hath bespoken mee."
Then ben Sir Tomas sore despight,
  And back unto his hall went hee
With face as ashen white.

V.

" O Robin, wilt thou wed this girl,
  Whenas she is so vaine a sprite? "
So spak ffull many an envious churle
  Unto that curteyse countrie wight.
But Robin did not pay no heede;
  And they ben wed a somer night
& danct upon ye meade.

VI.

Then scarse ben past a yeare & daye
   Whan Robin toke unto his bed,
And long, long time therein he lay,
   Nor colde not work to earn his bread ;
in soche an houre, whan times ben sore,
   Sr. Tomas came with haughtie tread
& knockit at ye doore.

VII.

Saies : " Madge, ye hoyden, do you know
   how that you once despighted me ?
But Ile forgiff an you will go
   my swete harte lady ffor to bee ! "
But Madge, ye hoyden, heard noe more, —
   straightway upon her heele turnt shee,
& shote ye cottage doore.

VIII.

Soe Madge, ye hoyden, did her parte
   whiles that ye years did come and go ;
't was somer allwais in her harte,
   tho' winter strewed her head with snowe.
She toilt and span thro' all those years
   nor bid repine that it ben soe,
nor never shad noe teares.

IX.

Whiles Robin lay within his bed,
   A divell came and whispered lowe, —
" Giff you will doe my will," he said,
   " None more of sickness you shall knowe ! "
Ye which gave joy to Robin's soul —
   Saies Robin : " Divell, be it soe,
an that you make me whoale ! "

X.

That day, upp rising ffrom his bed,
   Quoth Robin : " I am well again ! "
& backe he came as from ye dead,
   & he ben mickle blithe as when
he wooed his doxy long ago ;
   & Madge did make ado & then
Her teares ffor joy did flowe.

XI.

Then came that hell-born cloven thing —
   Saies : " Robin, I do claim your life,
and I hencefoorth shall be your king,
   and you shall do my evill strife.
Look round about and you shall see
   sr. Tomas' young and ffoolish wiffe —
a comely dame is shee ! "

XII.

Ye divell had him in his power,
    and not colde Robin say thereto:
Soe Robin from that very houre
    did what that divell bade him do;
He wooed and clipt, and on a daye
    sr. Tomas' wife and Robin flewe
a many leagues away.

XIII.

Sir Tomas ben wood wroth and swore,
    And sometime strode thro' leaf & brake
and knockit at ye cottage door
    and thus to Madge, ye hoyden, spake:
Saies, " I wolde have you ffor mine own,
    So come with mee & bee my make,
syn tother birds ben flown."

XIV.

But Madge, ye hoyden, bade him noe;
    Saies: " Robin is my swete harte still,
And, tho' he doth despight me soe,
    I mean to do him good for ill.
So goe, Sir Tomas, goe your way;
    ffor whiles I bee on live I will
ffor Robin's coming pray ! "

XV.

Soe Madge, ye hoyden, kneelt & prayed
    that Godde sholde send her Robin backe.
And tho' ye folke vast scoffing made,
    and tho' ye worlde ben colde and blacke,
And tho', as moneths dragged away,
    ye hoyden's harte ben like to crack
With griff, she still did praye.

XVI.

Sicke of that divell's damnèd charmes,
    Aback did Robin come at last,
And Madge, ye hoyden, sprad her arms
    and gave a cry and held him fast;
And as she clong to him and cried,
    her patient harte with joy did brast,
& Madge, ye hoyden, died.

OLD ENGLISH LULLABY.

HUSH, bonnie, dinna greit;
    Moder will rocke her sweete, —
      Balow, my boy!
When that his toile ben done,
Daddie will come anone, —
Hush thee, my lyttel one;
      Balow, my boy!

Gin thou dost sleepe, perchaunce
Fayries will come to daunce, —
      Balow, my boy!
Oft hath thy moder seene
Moonlight and mirkland queene
Daunce on thy slumbering een, —
      Balow, my boy!

Then droned a bomblebee
Saftly this songe to thee:
      " Balow, my boy!"

And a wee heather bell,
Pluckt from a fayry dell,
Chimed thee this rune hersell:
   " Balow, my boy ! "

Soe, bonnie, dinna greit;
Moder doth rock her sweete, —
   Balow, my boy !
Give mee thy lyttel hand,
Moder will hold it and
Lead thee to balow land, —
   Balow, my boy !

THE BIBLIOMANIAC'S PRAYER.

KEEP me, I pray, in wisdom's way
    That I may truths eternal seek ;
I need protecting care to-day, —
    My purse is light, my flesh is weak.
So banish from my erring heart
    All baleful appetites and hints
Of Satan's fascinating art,
    Of first editions, and of prints.
Direct me in some godly walk
    Which leads away from bookish strife,
That I with pious deed and talk
    May extra-illustrate my life.

But if, O Lord, it pleaseth Thee
    To keep me in temptation's way,
I humbly ask that I may be
    Most notably beset to-day ;
Let my temptation be a book,
    Which I shall purchase, hold, and keep,

Whereon when other men shall look,
They 'll wail to know I got it cheap.
Oh, let it such a volume be
As in rare copperplates abounds,
Large paper, clean, and fair to see,
Uncut, unique, unknown to Lowndes.

THE LYTTEL BOY.

SOMETIME there ben a lyttel boy
   That wolde not renne and play,
And helpless like that little tyke
   Ben allwais in the way.
" Goe, make you merrie with the rest,"
   His weary moder cried ;
But with a frown he catcht her gown
   And hong untill her side.

That boy did love his moder well,
   Which spake him faire, I ween ;
He loved to stand and hold her hand
   And ken her with his een ;
His cosset bleated in the croft,
   His toys unheeded lay, —
He wolde not goe, but, tarrying soe,
   Ben allwais in the way.

Godde loveth children and doth gird
   His throne with soche as these,
And He doth smile in plaisaunce while
   They cluster at His knees;
And sometime, when He looked on earth
   And watched the bairns at play,
He kenned with joy a lyttel boy
   Ben allwais in the way.

And then a moder felt her heart
   How that it ben to-torne, —
She kissed eche day till she ben gray
   The shoon he use to worn;
No bairn let hold untill her gown
   Nor played upon the floore, —
Godde's was the joy; a lyttel boy
   Ben in the way no more!

THE TRUTH ABOUT HORACE.

I T is very aggravating
    To hear the solemn prating
Of the fossils who are stating
    That old Horace was a prude;
When we know that with the ladies
He was always raising Hades,
And with many an escapade his
    Best productions are imbued.

There 's really not much harm in a
Large number of his carmina,
But these people find alarm in a
    Few records of his acts;
So they 'd squelch the muse caloric,
And to students sophomoric
They 'd present as metaphoric
    What old Horace meant for facts.

We have always thought 'em lazy;
Now we adjudge 'em crazy!
Why, Horace was a daisy
　　That was very much alive!
And the wisest of us know him
As his Lydia verses show him, —
Go, read that virile poem, —
　　It is No. 25.

He was a very owl, sir,
And starting out to prowl, sir,
You bet he made Rome howl, sir,
　　Until he filled his date;
With a massic-laden ditty
And a classic maiden pretty
He painted up the city,
　　And Mæcenas paid the freight!

THE DEATH OF ROBIN HOOD.

"GIVE me my bow," said Robin Hood,
    " An arrow give to me ;
And where 't is shot mark thou that spot,
    For there my grave shall be."

Then Little John did make no sign,
    And not a word he spake ;
But he smiled, altho' with mickle woe
    His heart was like to break.

He raised his master in his arms,
    And set him on his knee ;
And Robin's eyes beheld the skies,
    The shaws, the greenwood tree.

The brook was babbling as of old,
    The birds sang full and clear,
And the wild-flowers gay like a carpet lay
    In the path of the timid deer.

" O Little John," said Robin Hood,
  " Meseemeth now to be
Standing with you so stanch and true
  Under the greenwood tree.

" And all around I hear the sound
  Of Sherwood long ago,
And my merry men come back again, —
  You know, sweet friend, you know!

" Now mark this arrow; where it falls,
  When I am dead dig deep,
And bury me there in the greenwood where
  I would forever sleep."

He twanged his bow.   Upon its course
  The clothyard arrow sped,
And when it fell in yonder dell,
  Brave Robin Hood was dead.

The sheriff sleeps in a marble vault,
  The king in a shroud of gold;
And upon the air with a chanted pray'r
  Mingles the mock of mould.

But the deer draw to the shady pool,
    The birds sing blithe and free,
And the wild-flow'rs bloom o'er a hidden tomb
    Under the greenwood tree.

"LOLLYBY, LOLLY, LOLLYBY."

L AST night, whiles that the curfew bell ben
    ringing,
I heard a moder to her dearie singing
      " Lollyby, lolly, lollyby."
And presently that chylde did cease hys weeping,
And on his moder's breast did fall a-sleeping,
      To "lolly, lolly, lollyby."

Faire ben the chylde unto his moder clinging,
But fairer yet the moder's gentle singing, —
      " Lollyby, lolly, lollyby."
And angels came and kisst the dearie smiling
In dreems while him hys moder ben beguiling
      With "lolly, lolly, lollyby ! "

Then to my harte saies I, " Oh, that thy beating
Colde be assuaged by some swete voice repeating
      ' Lollyby, lolly, lollyby ; '

That like this lyttel chylde I, too, ben sleeping
With plaisaunt phantasies about me creeping,
      To 'lolly, lolly, lollyby !' "

Sometime — mayhap when curfew bells are ring-
      ing —
A weary harte shall heare straunge voices singing,
      "Lollyby, lolly, lollyby ; "
Sometime, mayhap, with Chrysts love round me
      streaming,
I shall be lulled into eternal dreeming
      With "lolly, lolly, lollyby."

HORACE AND LYDIA RECONCILED.

HORACE.

WHEN you were mine in auld lang syne,
 And when none else your charms might ogle,
  I 'll not deny,
  Fair nymph, that I
Was happier than a Persian mogul.

LYDIA.

Before *she* came — that rival flame ! —
 (Was ever female creature sillier ?)
  In those good times,
  Bepraised in rhymes,
I was more famed than Mother Ilia !

HORACE.

Chloe of Thrace !   With what a grace
 Does she at song or harp employ her !
  I 'd gladly die
  If only I
Might live forever to enjoy her !

LYDIA.

My Sybaris so noble is
  That, by the gods ! I love him madly —
    That I might save
    Him from the grave
  I 'd give my life, and give it gladly !

HORACE.

What if ma belle from favor fell,
  And I made up my mind to shake her,
    Would Lydia, then,
    Come back again
  And to her quondam flame betake her ?

LYDIA.

My other beau should surely go,
  And you alone should find me gracious ;
    For no one slings
    Such odes and things
  As does the lauriger Horatius !

OUR TWO OPINIONS.

US two wuz boys when we fell out, —
    Nigh to the age uv my youngest now;
Don't rec'lect what 't wuz about,
    Some small deeff'rence, I 'll allow.
Lived next neighbors twenty years,
    A-hatin' each other, me 'nd Jim, —
He havin' *his* opinyin uv *me*,
    'Nd *I* havin' *my* opinyin uv *him*.

Grew up together 'nd would n't speak,
    Courted sisters, 'nd marr'd 'em, too;
'Tended same meetin'-house oncet a week,
    A-hatin' each other through 'nd through!
But when Abe Linkern asked the West
    F'r soldiers, we answered, — me 'nd Jim, —
He havin' *his* opinyin uv *me*,
    'Nd *I* havin' *my* opinyin uv *him*.

But down in Tennessee one night
　　Ther wuz sound uv firin' fur away,
'Nd the sergeant allowed ther 'd be a fight
　　With the Johnnie Rebs some time nex' day;
'Nd as I wuz thinkin' uv Lizzie 'nd home
　　Jim stood afore me, long nd 'slim, —
He havin' *his* opinyin uv *me*,
　　'Nd *I* havin' *my* opinyin uv *him*.

Seemed like we knew there wuz goin' to be
　　Serious trouble f'r me 'nd him ;
Us two shuck hands, did Jim 'nd me,
　　But never a word from me or Jim !
He went *his* way 'nd *I* went *mine*,
　　'Nd into the battle's roar went we, —
I havin' *my* opinyin uv Jim,
　　'Nd *he* havin' *his* opinyin uv *me*.

Jim never come back from the war again,
　　But I haint forgot that last, last night
When, waitin' f'r orders, us two men
　　Made up 'nd shuck hands, afore the fight。
'Nd, after it all, it 's soothin' to know
　　That here *I* be 'nd yonder 's Jim, —
He havin' *his* opinyin uv *me*,
　　'Nd *I* havin' *my* opinyin uv *him*.

MOTHER AND CHILD.

ONE night a tiny dewdrop fell
    Into the bosom of a rose, —
" Dear little one, I love thee well,
    Be ever here thy sweet repose ! "

Seeing the rose with love bedight,
    The envious sky frowned dark, and then
Sent forth a messenger of light
    And caught the dewdrop up again.

" Oh, give me back my heavenly child, —
    My love ! " the rose in anguish cried ;
Alas ! the sky triumphant smiled,
    And so the flower, heart-broken, died.

3

ORKNEY LULLABY.

A MOONBEAM floateth from the skies,
    Whispering, " Heigho, my dearie !
I would spin a web before your eyes, —
A beautiful web of silver light,
Wherein is many a wondrous sight
Of a radiant garden leagues away,
Where the softly tinkling lilies sway,
And the snow-white lambkins are at play, —
    Heigho, my dearie ! "

A brownie stealeth from the vine
    Singing, " Heigho, my dearie !
And will you hear this song of mine, —
A song of the land of murk and mist
Where bideth the bud the dew hath kisst ?
Then let the moonbeam's web of light
Be spun before thee silvery white,
And I shall sing the livelong night, —
    Heigho, my dearie ! "

The night wind speedeth from the sea,
     Murmuring, " Heigho, my dearie !
I bring a mariner's prayer for thee ;
So let the moonbeam veil thine eyes,
And the brownie sing thee lullabies ;
But I shall rock thee to and fro,
Kissing the brow *he* loveth so,
And the prayer shall guard thy bed, I trow, —
     Heigho, my dearie ! "

LITTLE MACK.

THIS talk about the journalists that run the East
is bosh,
We 've got a Western editor that 's little, but, O
gosh !
He lives here in Mizzoora where the people are so
set
In ante-bellum notions that they vote for Jackson
yet;
But the paper he is running makes the rusty fossils
swear, —
The smartest, likeliest paper that is printed any-
where !
And, best of all, the paragraphs are pointed as a
tack,
And that 's because they emanate
From little Mack.

In architecture he is what you 'd call a chunky man,
As if he 'd been constructed on the summer-cottage
plan ;

He has a nose like Bonaparte; and round his mo-
    bile mouth
Lies all the sensuous languor of the children of the
    South;
His dealings with reporters who affect a weekly bust
Have given to his violet eyes a shadow of distrust;
In glorious abandon his brown hair wanders back
        From the grand Websterian forehead
            Of little Mack.

No matter what the item is, if there's an item in it,
You bet your life he's on to it and nips it in a
    minute!
From multifarious nations, countries, monarchies,
    and lands,
From Afric's sunny fountains and India's coral
    strands,
From Greenland's icy mountains and Siloam's
    shady rills,
He gathers in his telegrams, and Houser pays the
    bills;
What though there be a dearth of news, he has a
    happy knack
        Of scraping up a lot of scoops,
            Does little Mack.

And learning ?   Well he knows the folks of every
        tribe and age
That ever played a part upon this fleeting human
        stage ;
His intellectual system 's so extensive and so greedy
That, when it comes to records, he 's a walkin' cy-
        clopedy ;
For having studied (and digested) all the books
        a-goin',
It stands to reason he must know about all 's worth
        a-knowin' !
So when a politician with a record 's on the track,
        We 're apt to hear some history
          From little Mack.

And when a fellow-journalist is broke and needs a
        twenty,
Who 's allus ready to whack up a portion of his
        plenty ?
Who 's allus got a wallet that 's as full of sordid
        gain
As his heart is full of kindness and his head is full
        of brain ?
Whose bowels of compassion will in-va-ri-a-bly
        move

Their owner to those courtesies which plainly,
  surely prove
That he 's the kind of person that never does go
  back
      On a fellow that 's in trouble ?
      Why, little Mack !

I 've heard 'em tell of Dana, and of Bonner, and of
  Reid,
Of Johnnie Cockerill, who, I 'll own, is very smart
  indeed ;
Yet I don't care what their renown or influence
  may be,
One metropolitan exchange is quite enough for me !
So keep your Danas, Bonners, Reids, your Cock-
  erills, and the rest,
The woods is full of better men all through this
  woolly West;
For all that sleek, pretentious, Eastern editorial
  pack
      We would n't swap the shadow of
      Our little Mack !

TO ROBIN GOODFELLOW.

I SEE you, Maister Bawsy-brown,
   Through yonder lattice creepin';
You come for cream and to gar me dream,
   But you dinna find me sleepin'.
The moonbeam, that upon the floor
   Wi' crickets ben a-jinkin',
Now steals away fra' her bonnie play —
   Wi' a rosier blie, I 'm thinkin'.

I saw you, Maister Bawsy-brown,
   When the blue bells went a-ringin'
For the merrie fays o' the banks an' braes,
   And I kenned your bonnie singin';
The gowans gave you honey sweets,
   And the posies on the heather
Dript draughts o' dew for the faery crew
   That danct and sang together.

But posie-bloom an' simmer-dew
  And ither sweets o' faery
Cud na gae down wi' Bawsy-brown,
  Sae nigh to Maggie's dairy!
My pantry shelves, sae clean and white,
  Are set wi' cream and cheeses, —
Gae, gin you will, an' take your fill
  Of whatsoever pleases.

Then wave your wand aboon my een
  Until they close awearie,
And the night be past sae sweet and fast
  Wi' dreamings o' my dearie.
But pinch the wench in yonder room,
  For she's na gude nor bonnie, —
Her shelves be dust and her pans be rust,
  And she winkit at my Johnnie!

APPLE-PIE AND CHEESE.

FULL many a sinful notion
      Conceived of foreign powers
Has come across the ocean
    To harm this land of ours;
And heresies called fashions
    Have modesty effaced,
And baleful, morbid passions
    Corrupt our native taste.
O tempora! O mores!
    What profanations these
That seek to dim the glories
    Of apple-pie and cheese!

I 'm glad my education
    Enables me to stand
Against the vile temptation
    Held out on every hand:
Eschewing all the tittles
    With vanity replete,

I 'm loyal to the victuals
    Our grandsires used to eat!
I 'm glad I 've got three willing boys
    To hang around and tease
Their mother for the filling joys
    Of apple-pie and cheese!

Your flavored creams and ices
    And your dainty angel-food
Are mighty fine devices
    To regale the dainty dude;
Your terrapin and oysters,
    With wine to wash 'em down,
Are just the thing for roisters
    When painting of the town;
No flippant, sugared notion
    Shall *my* appetite appease,
Or bate my soul's devotion
    To apple-pie and cheese!

The pie my Julia makes me
    (God bless her Yankee ways!)
On memory's pinions takes me
    To dear Green Mountain days;

And seems like I saw Mother
    Lean on the window-sill,
A-handin' me and brother
    What she knows 'll keep us still;
And these feelings are so grateful,
    Says I, " Julia, if you please,
I 'll take another plateful
    Of that apple-pie and cheese!"

And cheese!   No alien it, sir,
    That's brought across the sea, —
No Dutch antique, nor Switzer,
    Nor glutinous de Brie;
There's nothing I abhor so
    As mawmets of this ilk —
Give *me* the harmless morceau
    That's made of true-blue milk!
No matter what conditions
    Dyspeptic come to feaze,
The best of all physicians
    Is apple-pie and cheese!

Though ribalds may decry 'em,
    For these twin boons we stand,
Partaking thrice per diem
    Of their fulness out of hand;

No enervating fashion
  Shall cheat us of our right
To gratify our passion
  With a mouthful at a bite!
We 'll cut it square or bias,
  Or any way we please,
And faith shall justify us
  When we carve our pie and cheese!

De gustibus, 't is stated,
  Non disputandum est.
Which meaneth, when translated,
  That all is for the best.
So let the foolish choose 'em
  The vapid sweets of sin,
I will not disabuse 'em
  Of the heresy they 're in;
But I, when I undress me
  Each night, upon my knees
Will ask the Lord to bless me
  With apple-pie and cheese!

KRINKEN.

KRINKEN was a little child, —
      It was summer when he smiled.
Oft the hoary sea and grim
Stretched its white arms out to him,
Calling, " Sun-child, come to me ;
Let me warm my heart with thee ! "
But the child heard not the sea,
Calling, yearning evermore
For the summer on the shore.

Krinken on the beach one day
Saw a maiden Nis at play ;
On the pebbly beach she played
In the summer Krinken made.
Fair, and very fair, was she,
Just a little child was he.

"Krinken," said the maiden Nis,
"Let me have a little kiss, —
Just a kiss, and go with me
To the summer-lands that be
Down within the silver sea."

Krinken was a little child —
By the maiden Nis beguiled,
Hand in hand with her went he,
And 't was summer in the sea.
And the hoary sea and grim
To its bosom folded him —
Clasped and kissed the little form,
And the ocean's heart was warm.

Now the sea calls out no more;
It is winter on the shore, —
Winter where that little child
Made sweet summer when he smiled;
Though 't is summer on the sea
Where with maiden Nis went he, —
Summer, summer evermore, —
It is winter on the shore,
Winter, winter evermore.

Of the summer on the deep
Come sweet visions in my sleep:
His fair face lifts from the sea,
His dear voice calls out to me, —
These my dreams of summer be.

Krinken was a little child,
By the maiden Nis beguiled;
Oft the hoary sea and grim
Reached its longing arms to him,
Crying, "Sun-child, come to me;
Let me warm my heart with thee!"
But the sea calls out no more;
It is winter on the shore, —
Winter, cold and dark and wild;
Krinken was a little child, —
It was summer when he smiled;
Down he went into the sea,
And the winter bides with me.
Just a little child was he.

BÉRANGER'S "BROKEN FIDDLE."

I.

THERE, there, poor dog, my faithful friend,
　　Pay you no heed unto my sorrow ·
But feast to-day while yet you may, —
　　Who knows but we shall starve to-morrow!

II.

"Give us a tune," the foemen cried,
　　In one of their profane caprices;
I bade them "No" — they frowned, and, lo!
　　They dashed this innocent in pieces!

III.

This fiddle was the village pride —
　　The mirth of every fête enhancing;
Its wizard art set every heart
　　As well as every foot to dancing.

4

IV.

How well the bridegroom knew its voice,
  As from its strings its song went gushing !
Nor long delayed the promised maid
  Equipped for bridal, coy and blushing.

V.

Why, it discoursed so merrily,
  It quickly banished all dejection ;
And yet, when pressed, our priest confessed
  I played with pious circumspection.

VI.

And though, in patriotic song,
  It was our guide, compatriot, teacher,
I never thought the foe had wrought
  His fury on the helpless creature !

VII.

But there, poor dog, my faithful friend,
  Pay you no heed unto my sorrow;
I prithee take this paltry cake, —
  Who knows but we shall starve to-morrow !

VIII.

Ah, who shall lead the Sunday choir
    As this old fiddle used to do it?
Can vintage come, with this voice dumb
    That used to bid a welcome to it?

IX.

It soothed the weary hours of toil,
    It brought forgetfulness to debtors;
Time and again from wretched men
    It struck oppression's galling fetters.

X.

No man could hear its voice, and hate;
    It stayed the teardrop at its portal;
With that dear thing I was a king
    As never yet was monarch mortal!

XI.

Now has the foe — the vandal foe —
    Struck from my hands their pride and glory;
There let it lie! In vengeance, I
    Shall wield another weapon, gory!

XII.

And if, O countrymen, I fall,
　Beside our grave let this be spoken:
" No foe of France shall ever dance
　Above the heart and fiddle, broken!"

XIII.

So come, poor dog, my faithful friend,
　I prithee do not heed my sorrow,
But feast to-day while yet you may,
　For we are like to starve to-morrow.

THE LITTLE PEACH.

A LITTLE peach in the orchard grew, —
   A little peach of emerald hue;
Warmed by the sun and wet by the dew,
         It grew.

One day, passing that orchard through,
That little peach dawned on the view
Of Johnny Jones and his sister Sue —
         Them two.

Up at that peach a club they threw —
Down from the stem on which it grew
Fell that peach of emerald hue.
         Mon Dieu!

John took a bite and Sue a chew,
And then the trouble began to brew, —
Trouble the doctor could n't subdue.
         Too true!

Under the turf where the daisies grew
They planted John and his sister Sue,
And their little souls to the angels flew, —
   Boo hoo!

What of that peach of the emerald hue,
Warmed by the sun, and wet by the dew?
Ah, well, its mission on earth is through.
   Adieu!

1880.

HORACE III. 13.

O FOUNTAIN of Bandusia,
　　Whence crystal waters flow,
With garlands gay and wine I 'll pay
　　The sacrifice I owe;
A sportive kid with budding horns
　　I have, whose crimson blood
Anon shall dye and sanctify
　　Thy cool and babbling flood.

O fountain of Bandusia,
　　The dogstar's hateful spell
No evil brings unto the springs
　　That from thy bosom well;
Here oxen, wearied by the plough,
　　The roving cattle here,
Hasten in quest of certain rest
　　And quaff thy gracious cheer.

O fountain of Bandusia,
   Ennobled shalt thou be,
For I shall sing the joys that spring
   Beneath yon ilex-tree;
Yes, fountain of Bandusia,
   Posterity shall know
The cooling brooks that from thy nooks
   Singing and dancing go!

THE DIVINE LULLABY.

I HEAR Thy voice, dear Lord;
  I hear it by the stormy sea
 When winter nights are black and wild,
And when, affright, I call to Thee;
It calms my fears and whispers me,
  "Sleep well, my child."

 I hear Thy voice, dear Lord,
In singing winds, in falling snow,
  The curfew chimes, the midnight bell.
"Sleep well, my child," it murmurs low;
"The guardian angels come and go, —
  O child, sleep well!"

 I hear Thy voice, dear Lord,
Ay, though the singing winds be stilled,
  Though hushed the tumult of the deep,
My fainting heart with anguish chilled
By Thy assuring tone is thrilled, —
  "Fear not, and sleep!"

Speak on — speak on, dear Lord!
And when the last dread night is near,
   With doubts and fears and terrors wild,
Oh, let my soul expiring hear
Only these words of heavenly cheer,
   "Sleep well, my child!"

IN THE FIRELIGHT.

THE fire upon the hearth is low,
　And there is stillness everywhere,
　While like winged spirits, here and there,
The firelight shadows fluttering go.
And as the shadows round me creep,
　A childish treble breaks the gloom,
　And softly from a further room
Comes, " Now I lay me down to sleep."

And somehow, with that little prayer
　And that sweet treble in my ears,
　My thoughts go back to distant years
And linger with a loved one there ;
And as I hear my child's amen,
　My mother's faith comes back to me, —
　Crouched at her side I seem to be,
And Mother holds my hands again.

Oh, for an hour in that dear place !
  Oh, for the peace of that dear time!
  Oh, for that childish trust sublime!
Oh, for a glimpse of Mother's face!
Yet, as the shadows round me creep,
  I do not seem to be alone, —
  Sweet magic of that treble tone,
And " Now I lay me down to sleep."

1885.

HEINE'S "WIDOW OR DAUGHTER?"

SHALL I woo the one or other?
    Both attract me — more 's the pity!
Pretty is the widowed mother,
    And the daughter, too, is pretty.

When I see that maiden shrinking,
    By the gods I swear I 'll get 'er!
But anon I fall to thinking
    That the mother 'll suit me better!

So, like any idiot ass
    Hungry for the fragrant fodder,
Placed between two bales of grass,
    Lo, I doubt, delay, and dodder!

CHRISTMAS TREASURES.

I COUNT my treasures o'er with care, —
    The little toy my darling knew,
    A little sock of faded hue,
A little lock of golden hair.

Long years ago this holy time,
    My little one — my all to me —
    Sat robed in white upon my knee
And heard the merry Christmas chime.

" Tell me, my little golden-head,
    If Santa Claus should come to-night,
    What shall he bring my baby bright, —
What treasure for my boy ? " I said.

And then he named this little toy,
    While in his round and mournful eyes
    There came a look of sweet surprise,
That spake his quiet, trustful joy.

And as he lisped his evening prayer
    He asked the boon with childish grace ,
    Then, toddling to the chimney-place,
He hung this little stocking there.

That night, while lengthening shadows crept,
    I saw the white-winged angels come
    With singing to our lowly home
And kiss my darling as he slept.

They must have heard his little prayer,
    For in the morn, with rapturous face,
    He toddled to the chimney-place,
And found this little treasure there.

They came again one Christmas-tide, —
    That angel host, so fair and white !
    And singing all that glorious night,
They lured my darling from my side.

A little sock, a little toy,
    A little lock of golden hair,
    The Christmas music on the air,
A watching for my baby boy!

But if again that angel train
    And golden-head come back for me,
    To bear me to Eternity,
My watching will not be in vain!

  1879.

DE AMICITIIS.

THOUGH care and strife
Elsewhere be rife,
Upon my word I do not heed 'em;
In bed I lie
With books hard by,
And with increasing zest I read 'em.

Propped up in bed,
So much I 've read
Of musty tomes that I 've a headful
Of tales and rhymes
Of ancient times,
Which, wife declares, are "simply dreadful!"

They give me joy
Without alloy;
And is n't that what books are made for?
And yet — and yet —
(Ah, vain regret!)
I would to God they all were paid for!

No festooned cup
Filled foaming up
Can lure me elsewhere to confound me;
Sweeter than wine
This love of mine
For these old books I see around me!

A plague, I say,
On maidens gay;
I 'll weave no compliments to tell 'em!
Vain fool I were,
Did I prefer
Those dolls to these old friends in vellum!

At dead of night
My chamber 's bright
Not only with the gas that 's burning,
But with the glow
Of long ago, —
Of beauty back from eld returning.

Fair women's looks
I see in books,
I see *them*, and I hear their laughter, —
Proud, high-born maids,
Unlike the jades
Which menfolk now go chasing after!

Herein again
Speak valiant men
Of all nativities and ages;
I hear and smile
With rapture while
I turn these musty, magic pages.

The sword, the lance,
The morris dance,
The highland song, the greenwood ditty,
Of these I read,
Or, when the need,
My Miller grinds me grist that's gritty!

When of such stuff
We've had enough,
Why, there be other friends to greet us;
We'll moralize
In solemn wise
With Plato or with Epictetus.

Sneer as you may,
I'm proud to say
That I, for one, am very grateful
To Heaven, that sends
These genial friends
To banish other friendships hateful!

And when I 'm done,
I 'd have no son
Pounce on these treasures like a vulture;
Nay, give them half
My epitaph,
And let them share in my sepulture.

Then, when the crack
Of doom rolls back
The marble and the earth that hide me,
I 'll smuggle home
Each precious tome,
Without a fear my wife shall chide me!

OUR LADY OF THE MINE.

THE Blue Horizon wuz a mine us fellers all
    thought well uv,
And there befell the episode I now perpose to
    tell uv;
'T wuz in the year uv sixty-nine, — somewhere
    along in summer, —
There hove in sight one afternoon a new and
    curious comer;
His name wuz Silas Pettibone, — a artist by per-
    fession, —
With a kit of tools and a big mustache and a
    pipe in his possession.
He told us, by our leave, he 'd kind uv like to
    make some sketches
Uv the snowy peaks, 'nd the foamin' crick, 'nd
    the distant mountain stretches;
" You 're welkim, sir," sez we, although this sce-
    nery dodge seemed to us
A waste uv time where scenery wuz already sooper-
    floo-us.

All through the summer Pettibone kep' busy at his
    sketchin', —

At daybreak off for Eagle Pass, and home at night-
    fall, fetchin'

That everlastin' book uv his with spider-lines all
    through it ;

Three-Fingered Hoover used to say there warn't
    no meanin' to it.

" Gol durn a man," sez he to him, " whose shif'less
    hand is sot at

A-drawin' hills that 's full uv quartz that 's pinin'
    to be got at ! "

" Go on," sez Pettibone, " go on, if joshin' grati-
    fies ye ;

But one uv these fine times I 'll show ye sumthin'
    will surprise ye ! "

The which remark led us to think — although he
    did n't say it —

That Pettibone wuz owin' us a gredge 'nd meant
    to pay it.

One evenin' as we sat around the Restauraw de
    Casey,

A-singin' songs 'nd tellin' yarns the which wuz
    sumwhat racy,

In come that feller Pettibone, 'nd sez, " With your
  permission,
I 'd like to put a picture I have made on exhi-
  bition."
He sot the picture on the bar 'nd drew aside its
  curtain,
Sayin', " I recken you 'll allow as how *that 's* art,
  f'r certain ! "
And then we looked, with jaws agape, but nary
  word wuz spoken,
And f'r a likely spell the charm uv silence wuz
  unbroken —
Till presently, as in a dream, remarked Three-
  Fingered Hoover :
" Onless I am mistaken, this is Pettibone's shef
  doover ! "

It wuz a face — a human face — a woman's, fair
  'nd tender —
Sot gracefully upon a neck white as a swan's, and
  slender ;
The hair wuz kind uv sunny, 'nd the eyes wuz sort
  uv dreamy,
The mouth wuz half a-smilin', 'nd the cheeks wuz
  soft 'nd creamy ;

It seemed like she wuz lookin' off into the west
 out yonder,
And seemed like, while she looked, we saw her
 eyes grow softer, fonder, —
Like, lookin' off into the west, where mountain
 mists wuz fallin',
She saw the face she longed to see and heerd his
 voice a-callin';
" Hooray ! " we cried, — "a woman in the camp uv
 Blue Horizon !
Step right up, Colonel Pettibone, 'nd nominate your
 pizen ! "

A curious situation, — one deservin' uv your
 pity, —
No human, livin', female thing this side of Denver
 City !
But jest a lot uv husky men that lived on sand 'nd
 bitters, —
Do you wonder that that woman's face consoled
 the lonesome critters ?
And not a one but what it served in some way to
 remind him
Of a mother or a sister or a sweetheart left behind
 him ;

And some looked back on happier days, and saw
the old-time faces
And heerd the dear familiar sounds in old familiar
places, —
A gracious touch of home. " Look here," sez
Hoover, " ever'body
Quit thinkin' 'nd perceed at oncet to name his
favorite toddy ! "

It wuz n't long afore the news had spread the coun-
try over,
And miners come a-flockin' in like honey-bees to
clover ;
It kind uv did 'em good, they said, to feast their
hungry eyes on
That picture uv Our Lady in the camp uv Blue
Horizon.
But one mean cuss from Nigger Crick passed criti-
cisms on 'er, —
Leastwise we overheerd him call her Pettibone's
madonner,
The which we did not take to be respectful to a
lady,
So we hung him in a quiet spot that wuz cool 'nd
dry 'nd shady;

Which same might not have been good law, but it
    wuz the right maneuver
To give the critics due respect for Pettibone's shef
    doover.

Gone is the camp, — yes, years ago the Blue Hori-
    zon busted,
And every mother's son uv us got up one day 'nd
    dusted,
While Pettibone perceeded East with wealth in his
    possession,
And went to Yurrup, as I heerd, to study his per-
    fession ;
So, like as not, you 'll find him now a-paintin' heads
    'nd faces
At Venus, Billy Florence, and the like I-talyun
    places.
But no sech face he 'll paint again as at old Blue
    Horizon,
For I 'll allow no sweeter face no human soul sot
    eyes on ;
And when the critics talk so grand uv Paris 'nd the
    Loover,
I say, " Oh, but you orter seen the Pettibone shef
    doover ! "

THE WANDERER.

UPON a mountain height, far from the sea,
  I found a shell,
And to my listening ear the lonely thing
Ever a song of ocean seemed to sing,
  Ever a tale of ocean seemed to tell.

How came the shell upon that mountain height?
  Ah, who can say
Whether there dropped by some too careless hand,
Or whether there cast when Ocean swept the Land,
  Ere the Eternal had ordained the Day?

Strange, was it not? Far from its native deep,
  One song it sang, —
Sang of the awful mysteries of the tide,
Sang of the misty sea, profound and wide, —
  Ever with echoes of the ocean rang.

And as the shell upon the mountain height
    Sings of the sea,
So do I ever, leagues and leagues away, —
So do I ever, wandering where I may, —
    Sing, O my home! sing, O my home! of thee.

1883.

TO A USURPER.

AHA! a traitor in the camp,
  A rebel strangely bold, —
A lisping, laughing, toddling scamp,
  Not more than four years old!

To think that I, who 've ruled alone
  So proudly in the past,
Should be ejected from my throne
  By my own son at last!

He trots his treason to and fro,
  As only babies can,
And says he 'll be his mamma's beau
  When he 's a " gweat, big man " !

You stingy boy! you 've always had
  A share in mamma's heart;
Would you begrudge your poor old dad
  The tiniest little part?

That mamma, I regret to see,
　　Inclines to take your part, —
As if a dual monarchy
　　Should rule her gentle heart !

But when the years of youth have sped,
　　The bearded man, I trow,
Will quite forget he ever said
　　He 'd be his mamma's beau.

Renounce your treason, little son,
　　Leave mamma's heart to me ;
For there will come another one
　　To claim your loyalty.

And when that other comes to you,
　　God grant her love may shine
Through all your life, as fair and true
　　As mamma's does through mine !

1885.

LULLABY; BY THE SEA.

FAIR is the castle up on the hill —
    Hushaby, sweet my own!
The night is fair, and the waves are still,
And the wind is singing to you and to me
In this lowly home beside the sea —
    Hushaby, sweet my own!

On yonder hill is store of wealth —
    Hushaby, sweet my own!
And revellers drink to a little one's health;
But you and I bide night and day
For the other love that has sailed away —
    Hushaby, sweet my own!

See not, dear eyes, the forms that creep
    Ghostlike, O my own!
Out of the mists of the murmuring deep;
Oh, see them not and make no cry
Till the angels of death have passed us by —
    Hushaby, sweet my own!

Ah, little they reck of you and me —
    Hushaby, sweet my own!
In our lonely home beside the sea;
They seek the castle up on the hill,
And there they will do their ghostly will —
    Hushaby, O my own!

Here by the sea a mother croons
    "Hushaby, sweet my own!"
In yonder castle a mother swoons
While the angels go down to the misty deep,
Bearing a little one fast asleep —
    Hushaby, sweet my own!

SOLDIER, MAIDEN, AND FLOWER.

" SWEETHEART, take this," a soldier said,
    "And bid me brave good-by ;
It may befall we ne'er shall wed,
    But love can never die.
Be steadfast in thy troth to me,
    And then, whate'er my lot,
' My soul to God, my heart to thee,' —
    Sweetheart, forget me not ! "

The maiden took the tiny flower
    And nursed it with her tears :
Lo ! he who left her in that hour
    Came not in after years.
Unto a hero's death he rode
    'Mid shower of fire and shot ;
But in the maiden's heart abode
    The flower, forget-me-not.

6

And when *he* came not with the rest
    From out the years of blood,
Closely unto her widowed breast
    She pressed a faded bud ;
Oh, there is love and there is pain,
    And there is peace, God wot, —
And these dear three do live again
    In sweet forget-me-not.

'T is to an unmarked grave to-day
    That I should love to go, —
Whether he wore the blue or gray,
    What need that we should know.
" He loved a woman," let us say,
    And on that sacred spot,
To woman's love, that lives for aye,
    We 'll strew forget-me-not.

1887.

HORACE TO MELPOMENE.

LOFTY and enduring is the monument I 've
    reared, —
  Come, tempests, with your bitterness assailing;
And thou, corrosive blasts of time, by all things
        mortal feared,
  Thy buffets and thy rage are unavailing!

I shall not altogether die; by far my greater part
  Shall mock man's common fate in realms infernal;
My works shall live as tributes to my genius and
        my art, —
  My works shall be my monument eternal!

While this great Roman empire stands and gods
        protect our fanes,
  Mankind with grateful hearts shall tell the story,
How one most lowly born upon the parched Apu-
        lian plains
  First raised the native lyric muse to glory.

Assume, revered Melpomene, the proud estate I 've
      won,
    And, with thine own dear hand the meed sup-
      plying,
Bind thou about the forehead of thy celebrated son
    The Delphic laurel-wreath of fame undying !

AILSIE, MY BAIRN.

LIE in my arms, Ailsie, my bairn, —
    Lie in my arms and dinna greit;
Long time been past syn I kenned you last,
    But my harte been allwais the same, my swete.

Ailsie, I colde not say you ill,
    For out of the mist of your bitter tears,
And the prayers that rise from your bonnie eyes
    Cometh a promise of oder yeres.

I mind the time when we lost our bairn, —
    Do you ken that time ? A wambling tot,
You wandered away ane simmer day,
    And we hunted and called, and found you not.

I promised God, if He 'd send you back,
    Alwaies to keepe and to love you, childe ;
And I 'm thinking again of that promise when
    I see you creep out of the storm sae wild.

You came back then as you come back now, —
    Your kirtle torn and your face all white;
And you stood outside and knockit and cried,
    Just as you, dearie, did to-night.

Oh, never a word of the cruel wrang,
    That has faded your cheek and dimmed your ee;
And never a word of the fause, fause lord, —
    Only a smile and a kiss for me.

Lie in my arms, as long, long syne,
    And sleepe on my bosom, deere wounded thing, —
I 'm nae sae glee as I use to be,
    Or I 'd sing you the songs I use to sing.

But Ile kemb my fingers thro' yr haire,
    And nane shall know, but you and I,
Of the love and the faith that came to us baith
    When Ailsie, my bairn, came home to die.

CORNISH LULLABY.

OUT on the mountain over the town,
    All night long, all night long,
The trolls go up and the trolls go down,
   Bearing their packs and crooning a song;
And this is the song the hill-folk croon,
As they trudge in the light of the misty moon, —
This is ever their dolorous tune :
" Gold, gold ! ever more gold, —
    Bright red gold for dearie ! "

Deep in the hill the yeoman delves
   All night long, all night long;
None but the peering, furtive elves
   See his toil and hear his song;
Merrily ever the cavern rings
As merrily ever his pick he swings,
And merrily ever this song he sings :
" Gold, gold ! ever more gold, —
    Bright red gold for dearie ! "

Mother is rocking thy lowly bed
    All night long, all night long,
Happy to smooth thy curly head
    And to hold thy hand and to sing her song ;
'T is not of the hill-folk, dwarfed and old,
Nor the song of the yeoman, stanch and bold,
And the burden it beareth is not of gold ;
But it 's " Love, love ! — nothing but love, —
      Mother's love for dearie ! "

UHLAND'S "THREE CAVALIERS."

THERE were three cavaliers that went over the
     Rhine,
And gayly they called to the hostess for wine.
" And where is thy daughter ? We would she were
     here, —
Go fetch us that maiden to gladden our cheer ! "

" I 'll fetch thee thy goblets full foaming," she
     said,
" But in yon darkened chamber the maiden lies
     dead."
And lo ! as they stood in the doorway, the white
Of a shroud and a dead shrunken face met their
     sight.

Then the first cavalier breathed a pitiful sigh,
And the throb of his heart seemed to melt in his
     eye,

And he cried, "Hadst thou lived, O my pretty
    white rose,
I ween I had loved thee and wed thee — who
    knows?"

The next cavalier drew aside a small space,
And stood to the wall with his hands to his face
And this was the heart-cry that came with his
    tears :
"I loved her, I loved her these many long years!"

But the third cavalier kneeled him down in that
    place,
And, as it were holy, he kissed that dead face:
"I loved thee long years, and I love thee to-day,
And I 'll love thee, dear maiden, forever and aye!"

A CHAUCERIAN PARAPHRASE OF HORACE.

SYN that you, Chloe, to your moder sticken,
 Maketh all ye yonge bacheloures full sicken;
Like as a lyttel deere you ben y-hiding
Whenas come lovers with theyre pityse chiding;
Sothly it ben faire to give up your moder
For to beare swete company with some oder;
Your moder ben well enow so farre shee goeth,
But that ben not farre enow, God knoweth;
Wherefore it ben sayed that foolysh ladyes
That marrye not shall leade an aype in Hadys;
But all that do with gode men wed full quickylye
When that they be on dead go to ye seints full
 sickerly.

NORSE LULLABY.

THE sky is dark and the hills are white
    As the storm-king speeds from the north
        to-night,
And this is the song the storm-king sings,
As over the world his cloak he flings :
    " Sleep, sleep, little one, sleep ; "
He rustles his wings and gruffly sings :
    " Sleep, little one, sleep."

On yonder mountain-side a vine
Clings at the foot of a mother pine ;
The tree bends over the trembling thing,
And only the vine can hear her sing :
    " Sleep, sleep, little one, sleep ;
What shall you fear when I am here ?
    Sleep, little one, sleep."

The king may sing in his bitter flight,
The tree may croon to the vine to-night,
But the little snowflake at my breast
Liketh the song *I* sing the best, —
    Sleep, sleep, little one, sleep ;
Weary thou art, anext my heart
    Sleep, little one, sleep.

BÉRANGER'S " MY LAST SONG PERHAPS."

[JANUARY, 1814.]

WHEN, to despoil my native France,
 With flaming torch and cruel sword
And boisterous drums her foeman comes,
 I curse him and his vandal horde !
Yet, what avail accrues to her,
 If we assume the garb of woe ?
Let 's merry be, — in laughter we
 May rescue somewhat from the foe !

Ah, many a brave man trembles now.
 I (coward !) show no sign of fear ;
When Bacchus sends his blessing, friends,
 I drown my panic in his cheer.
Come, gather round my humble board,
 And let the sparkling wassail flow, —
Chuckling to think, the while you drink,
 " This much we rescue from the foe ! "

My creditors beset me so
    And so environed my abode,
That I agreed, despite my need,
    To settle up the debts I owed;
When suddenly there came the news
    Of this invasion, as you know;
I 'll pay no score; pray, lend me more, —
    I — *I* will keep it from the foe!

Now here 's my mistress, — pretty dear! —
    Feigns terror at this martial noise,
And yet, methinks, the artful minx
    Would like to meet those soldier boys!
I tell her that they 're coarse and rude,
    Yet feel she don't believe 'em so, —
Well, never mind; so she be kind,
    That much I rescue from the foe!

If, brothers, hope shall have in store
    For us and ours no friendly glance,
Let 's rather die than raise a cry
    Of welcome to the foes of France!
But, like the swan that dying sings,
    Let us, O Frenchmen, singing go, —
Then shall our cheer, when death is near,
    Be so much rescued from the foe!

MR. DANA, OF THE NEW YORK SUN.

THAR showed up out 'n Denver in the spring
     uv '81
A man who 'd worked with Dana on the Noo York
     Sun.
His name wuz Cantell Whoppers, 'nd he wuz a
     sight ter view
Ez he walked inter the orfice 'nd inquired fer work
     to do.
Thar warn't no places vacant then, — fer be it un-
     derstood,
That wuz the time when talent flourished at that
     altitood;
But thar the stranger lingered, tellin' Raymond 'nd
     the rest
Uv what perdigious wonders he could do when at
     his best,
'Till finally he stated (quite by chance) that he hed
     done
A heap uv work with Dana on the Noo York Sun.

Wall, that wuz quite another thing; we owned that
    ary cuss

Who 'd worked f'r Mr. Dana *must* be good enough
    fer *us !*

And so we tuk the stranger's word 'nd nipped him
    while we could,

For if *we did n't* take him we knew John Arkins
    would ;

And Cooper, too, wuz mouzin' round fer enterprise
    'nd brains,

Whenever them commodities blew in across the
    plains.

At any rate we nailed him, which made ol' Cooper
    swear

And Arkins tear out handfuls uv his copious curly
    hair;

But *we* set back and cackled, 'nd hed a power uv
    fun

With our man who 'd worked with Dana on the Noo
    York Sun.

It made our eyes hang on our cheeks 'nd lower
    jaws ter drop,

Ter hear that feller tellin' how ol' Dana run his
    shop :

7

It seems that Dana wuz the biggest man you ever
 saw, —
He lived on human bein's, 'nd preferred to eat 'em
 raw !
If he hed democratic drugs ter take, before he took
 em',
As good old allopathic laws prescribe, he allus
 shook 'em.
The man that could set down 'nd write like Dany
 never grew,
And the sum of human knowledge wuz n't half
 what Dana knew;
The consequence appeared to be that nearly every
 one
Concurred with Mr. Dana of the Noo York Sun.

This feller, Cantell Whoppers, never brought an
 item in, —
He spent his time at Perrin's shakin' poker dice f'r
 gin.
Whatever the assignment he wuz allus sure to shirk,
He wuz very long on likker and all-fired short on
 work !
If any other cuss had played the tricks he dared
 ter play,

The daisies would be bloomin' over his remains
    to-day;
But somehow folks respected him and stood him
    to the last,
Considerin' his superior connections in the past.
So, when he bilked at poker, not a sucker drew a
    gun
On the man who 'd worked with Dana on the Noo
    York Sun.

Wall, Dana came ter Denver in the fall uv '83,
A very different party from the man we thought ter
    see, —
A nice 'nd clean old gentleman, so dignerfied 'nd
    calm,
You bet yer life he never did no human bein' harm!
A certain hearty manner 'nd a fulness uv the vest
Betokened that his sperrits 'nd his victuals wuz the
    best;
His face was so benevolent, his smile so sweet 'nd
    kind,
That they seemed to be the reflex uv an honest,
    healthy mind;
And God had set upon his head a crown uv silver
    hair

In promise uv the golden crown He meaneth him
    to wear.
So, uv us boys that met him out 'n Denver, there
    wuz none
But fell in love with Dana uv the Noo York
    Sun.

But when he came to Denver in that fall uv '83,
His old friend Cantell Whoppers disappeared
    upon a spree;
The very thought uv seein' Dana worked upon
    him so
(They had n't been together fer a year or two, you
    know),
That he borrered all the stuff he could and started
    on a bat,
And, strange as it may seem, we did n't see him
    after that.
So, when ol' Dana hove in sight, we could n't un-
    derstand
Why he did n't seem to notice that his crony wa' n't
    on hand;
No casual allusion, not a question, no, not one,
For the man who 'd " worked with Dana on the Noo
    York Sun!"

We broke it gently to him, but he did n't seem
surprised,
Thar wuz no big burst uv passion as we fellers had
surmised.
He said that Whoppers wuz a man he 'd never
heerd about,
But he mought have carried papers on a Jarsey
City route ;
And then he recollected hearin' Mr. Laffan say
That he 'd fired a man named Whoppers fur bein'
drunk one day,
Which, with more likker *underneath* than money *in*
his vest,
Had started on a freight train fur the great 'nd
boundin' West,
But further information or statistics he had none
Uv the man who 'd "worked with Dana on the Noo
York Sun."

We dropped the matter quietly 'nd never made no
fuss, —
When we get played for suckers, why, that 's a horse
on us ! —
But every now 'nd then we Denver fellers have to
laff

To hear some other paper boast uv havin' on its
   staff
A man who's "worked with Dana," 'nd then we
   fellers wink
And pull our hats down on our eyes 'nd set around
   'nd think.
It seems like Dana could n't be as smart as people
   say,
If he educates so many folks 'nd lets 'em get
   away;
And, as for us, in future we'll be very apt to
   shun
The man who "worked with Dana on the Noo
   York Sun."

But bless ye, Mr. Dana! may you live a thousan'
   years,
To sort o' keep things lively in this vale of human
   tears ;
An' may *I* live a thousan', too, — a thousan' less a
   day,
For I should n't like to be on earth to hear you'd
   passed away.
And when it comes your time to go you'll need no
   Latin chaff

Nor biographic data put in your epitaph;

But one straight line of English and of truth will
let folks know

The homage 'nd the gratitude 'nd reverence they
owe;

You'll need no epitaph but this: "Here sleeps
the man who run

That best 'nd brightest paper, the Noo York
Sun."

SICILIAN LULLABY.

HUSH, little one, and fold your hands;
        The sun hath set, the moon is high;
The sea is singing to the sands,
        And wakeful posies are beguiled
        By many a fairy lullaby:
        Hush, little child, my little child!

Dream, little one, and in your dreams
        Float upward from this lowly place, —
Float out on mellow, misty streams
        To lands where bideth Mary mild,
        And let her kiss thy little face,
        You little child, my little child!

Sleep, little one, and take thy rest,
        With angels bending over thee, —
Sleep sweetly on that Father's breast
        Whom our dear Christ hath reconciled;
        But stay not there, — come back to me,
        O little child, my little child!

HORACE TO PYRRHA.

WHAT perfumed, posie-dizened sirrah,
    With smiles for diet,
Clasps you, O fair but faithless Pyrrha,
    On the quiet?
For whom do you bind up your tresses,
    As spun-gold yellow, —
Meshes that go, with your caresses,
    To snare a fellow?

How will he rail at fate capricious,
    And curse you duly!
Yet now he deems your wiles delicious,
    You perfect, truly!
Pyrrha, your love's a treacherous ocean;
    He'll soon fall in there!
Then shall I gloat on his commotion,
    For *I* have been there!

THE TWENTY-THIRD PSALM.

MY Shepherd is the Lord my God, —
    There is no want I know;
His flock He leads in verdant meads,
    Where tranquil waters flow.

He doth restore my fainting soul
    With His divine caress,
And, when I stray, He points the way
    To paths of righteousness.

Yea, though I walk the vale of death,
    What evil shall I fear?
Thy staff and rod are mine, O God,
    And Thou, my Shepherd, near!

Mine enemies behold the feast
    Which my dear Lord hath spread;
And, lo! my cup He filleth up,
    With oil anoints my head!

Goodness and mercy shall be mine
   Unto my dying day ;
Then will I bide at His dear side
   Forever and for aye !

THE BIBLIOMANIAC'S BRIDE.

THE womenfolk are like to books, —
　　Most pleasing to the eye,
Whereon if anybody looks
　　He feels disposed to buy.

I hear that many are for sale, —
　　Those that record no dates,
And such editions as regale
　　The view with colored plates.

Of every quality and grade
　　And size they may be found, —
Quite often beautifully made,
　　As often poorly bound.

Now, as for me, had I my choice,
　　I 'd choose no folio tall,
But some octavo to rejoice
　　My sight and heart withal, —

As plump and pudgy as a snipe;
   Well worth her weight in gold;
Of honest, clean, conspicuous type,
   And *just* the size to hold!

With such a volume for my wife,
   How should I keep and con!
How like a dream should run my life
   Unto its colophon!

Her frontispiece should be more fair
   Than any colored plate;
Blooming with health, she would not care
   To extra-illustrate.

And in her pages there should be
   A wealth of prose and verse,
With now and then a *jeu d'esprit*, —
   But nothing ever worse!

Prose for me when I wished for prose,
   Verse when to verse inclined, —
Forever bringing sweet repose
   To body, heart, and mind.

Oh, I should bind this priceless prize
   In bindings full and fine,
And keep her where no human eyes
   Should see her charms, but mine!

With such a fair unique as this
   What happiness abounds!
Who — who could paint my rapturous bliss,
   My joy unknown to Lowndes!

CHRISTMAS HYMN.

SING, Christmas bells !
Say to the earth this is the morn
Whereon our Saviour-King is born;
   Sing to all men, — the bond, the free
The rich, the poor, the high, the low,
   The little child that sports in glee,
The aged folk that tottering go, —
      Proclaim the morn
      That Christ is born,
   That saveth them and saveth me !

      Sing, angel host !
Sing of the star that God has placed
Above the manger in the east;
   Sing of the glories of the night,
The virgin's sweet humility,
   The Babe with kingly robes bedight, —
Sing to all men where'er they be
      This Christmas morn;
      For Christ is born,
   That saveth them and saveth me !

Sing, sons of earth !
O ransomed seed of Adam, sing !
God liveth, and we have a king !
  The curse is gone, the bond are free, —
By Bethlehem's star that brightly beamed,
  By all the heavenly signs that be,
We know that Israel is redeemed ;
    That on this morn
    The Christ is born
  That saveth you and saveth me !

Sing, O my heart !
Sing thou in rapture this dear morn
Whereon the blessed Prince is born !
  And as thy songs shall be of love,
So let my deeds be charity, —
  By the dear Lord that reigns above,
By Him that died upon the tree,
    By this fair morn
    Whereon is born
  The Christ that saveth all and me !

JAPANESE LULLABY.

SLEEP, little pigeon, and fold your wings, —
  Little blue pigeon with velvet eyes ;
Sleep to the singing of mother-bird swinging —
  Swinging the nest where her little one lies.

Away out yonder I see a star, —
  Silvery star with a tinkling song ;
To the soft dew falling I hear it calling —
  Calling and tinkling the night along.

In through the window a moonbeam comes, —
  Little gold moonbeam with misty wings ;
All silently creeping, it asks, " Is he sleeping —
  Sleeping and dreaming while mother sings ? "

Up from the sea there floats the sob
  Of the waves that are breaking upon the shore,
As though they were groaning in anguish, and
      moaning —
  Bemoaning the ship that shall come no more.

8

But sleep, little pigeon, and fold your wings, —
Little blue pigeon with mournful eyes ;
Am I not singing ? — see, I am swinging —
Swinging the nest where my darling lies.

"GOOD-BY — GOD BLESS YOU!

I LIKE the Anglo-Saxon speech
   With its direct revealings;
It takes a hold, and seems to reach
   Way down into your feelings;
That some folk deem it rude, I know,
   And therefore they abuse it;
But I have never found it so, —
   Before all else I choose it.
I don't object that men should air
   The Gallic they have paid for,
With " Au revoir," " Adieu, ma chere,"
   For that 's what French was made for.
But when a crony takes your hand
   At parting, to address you,
He drops all foreign lingo and
   He says, " Good-by — God bless you!

This seems to me a sacred phrase,
   With reverence impassioned, —

A thing come down from righteous days,
  Quaintly but nobly fashioned ;
It well becomes an honest face,
  A voice that 's round and cheerful ;
It stays the sturdy in his place,
  And soothes the weak and fearful.
Into the porches of the ears
  It steals with subtle unction,
And in your heart of hearts appears
  To work its gracious function ;
And all day long with pleasing song
  It lingers to caress you, —
I 'm sure no human heart goes wrong
  That 's told " Good-by — God bless you ! "

I love the words, — perhaps because,
  When I was leaving Mother,
Standing at last in solemn pause
  We looked at one another,
And I — I saw in Mother's eyes
  The love she could not tell me, —
A love eternal as the skies,
  Whatever fate befell me ;
She put her arms about my neck
  And soothed the pain of leaving,

And though her heart was like to break,
    She spoke no word of grieving;
She let no tear bedim her eye,
    For fear *that* might distress me,
But, kissing me, she said good-by,
    And asked our God to bless me.

HORACE TO PHYLLIS.

COME, Phyllis, I 've a cask of wine
    That fairly reeks with precious juices,
And in your tresses you shall twine
    The loveliest flowers this vale produces.

My cottage wears a gracious smile, —
    The altar, decked in floral glory,
Yearns for the lamb which bleats the while
    As though it pined for honors gory.

Hither our neighbors nimbly fare, —
    The boys agog, the maidens snickering;
And savory smells possess the air
    As skyward kitchen flames are flickering.

You ask what means this grand display,
    This festive throng, and goodly diet?
Well, since you 're bound to have your way,
    I don't mind telling, on the quiet.

'T is April 13, as you know, —
    A day and month devote to Venus,
Whereon was born, some years ago,
    My very worthy friend Mæcenas.

Nay, pay no heed to Telephus, —
    Your friends agree he does n't love **you**;
The way he flirts convinces us
    He really is not worthy of you!

Aurora's son, unhappy lad!
    You know the fate that overtook him?
And Pegasus a rider had —
    I say he *had* before he shook him!

Hæc docet (as you must agree):
    'T is meet that Phyllis should discover
A wisdom in preferring me
    And mittening every other lover.

So come, O Phyllis, last and best
    Of loves with which this heart 's been smitten, —
Come, sing my jealous fears to rest,
    And let your songs be those *I 've* written.

CHRYSTMASSE OF OLDE.

GOD rest you, Chrysten gentil men,
　Wherever you may be, —
God rest you all in fielde or hall,
　Or on ye stormy sea ;
For on this morn oure Chryst is born
　That saveth you and me.

Last night ye shepherds in ye east
　Saw many a wondrous thing ;
Ye sky last night flamed passing bright
　Whiles that ye stars did sing,
And angels came to bless ye name
　Of Jesus Chryst, oure Kyng.

God rest you, Chrysten gentil men,
　Faring where'er you may ;
In noblesse court do thou no sport,
　In tournament no playe,
In paynim lands hold thou thy hands
　From bloudy works this daye.

But thinking on ye gentil Lord
   That died upon ye tree,
Let troublings cease and deeds of peace
   Abound in Chrystantie ;
For on this morn ye Chryst is born
   That saveth you and me.

AT THE DOOR.

I THOUGHT myself indeed secure,
　　So fast the door, so firm the lock;
But, lo! he toddling comes to lure
　　My parent ear with timorous knock.

My heart were stone could it withstand
　　The sweetness of my baby's plea, —
That timorous, baby knocking and
　　" Please let me in, — it 's only me."

I threw aside the unfinished book,
　　Regardless of its tempting charms,
And opening wide the door, I took
　　My laughing darling in my arms.

Who knows but in Eternity,
　　I, like a truant child, shall wait
The glories of a life to be,
　　Beyond the Heavenly Father's gate?

And will that Heavenly Father heed
    The truant's supplicating cry,
As at the outer door I plead,
    " 'T is I, O Father! only I ? "

1886.

HI-SPY.

STRANGE that the city thoroughfare,
  Noisy and bustling all the day,
Should with the night renounce its care
  And lend itself to children's play !

Oh, girls are girls, and boys are boys,
  And have been so since Abel's birth,
And shall be so 'til dolls and toys
  Are with the children swept from earth.

The self-same sport that crowns the day
  Of many a Syrian shepherd's son,
Beguiles the little lads at play
  By night in stately Babylon.

I hear their voices in the street,
  Yet 't is so different now from then !
Come, brother ! from your winding sheet,
  And let us two be boys again !

1886.

LITTLE CROODLIN DOO.

HO, pretty bee, did you see my croodlin doo?
    Ho, little lamb, is she jinkin' on the lea?
  Ho, bonnie fairy, bring my dearie back to me —
Got a lump o' sugar an' a posie for you,
Only bring back my wee, wee croodlin doo!

Why, here you are, my little croodlin doo!
    Looked in er cradle, but did n't find you there,
    Looked f'r my wee, wee croodlin doo ever'where;
Ben kind lonesome all er day withouten you;
Where you ben, my little wee, wee croodlin doo?

Now you go balow, my little croodlin doo;
    Now you go rockaby ever so far, —
    Rockaby, rockaby, up to the star
That's winkin' an' blinkin' an' singin' to you
As you go balow, my wee, wee croodlin doo!

THE "HAPPY ISLES" OF HORACE.

OH, come with me to the Happy Isles
   In the golden haze off yonder,
Where the song of the sun-kissed breeze beguiles,
   And the ocean loves to wander.

Fragrant the vines that mantle those hills,
   Proudly the fig rejoices ;
Merrily dance the virgin rills,
   Blending their myriad voices.

Our herds shall fear no evil there,
   But peacefully feed and rest them ;
Neither shall serpent or prowling bear
   Ever come there to molest them.

Neither shall Eurus, wanton bold,
   Nor feverish drouth distress us,
But he that compasseth heat and cold
   Shall temper them both to bless us.

There no vandal foot has trod,
  And the pirate hosts that wander
Shall never profane the sacred sod
  Of those beautiful Isles out yonder.

Never a spell shall blight our vines,
  Nor Sirius blaze above us,
But you and I shall drink our wines
  And sing to the loved that love us.

So come with me where Fortune smiles
  And the gods invite devotion, —
Oh, come with me to the Happy Isles
  In the haze of that far-off ocean !

DUTCH LULLABY.

WYNKEN, Blynken, and Nod one night
    Sailed off in a wooden shoe, —
Sailed on a river of misty light
    Into a sea of dew.
"Where are you going, and what do you wish ?
    The old moon asked the three.
"We have come to fish for the herring-fish
    That live in this beautiful sea ;
    Nets of silver and gold have we,"
        Said Wynken,
        Blynken,
        And Nod.

The old moon laughed and sung a song,
    As they rocked in the wooden shoe ;
And the wind that sped them all night long
    Ruffled the waves of dew ;
The little stars were the herring-fish
That lived in the beautiful sea.

" Now cast your nets wherever you wish,
  But never afeard are we ! "
So cried the stars to the fishermen three,
            Wynken,
            Blynken,
            And Nod.

All night long their nets they threw
  For the fish in the twinkling foam,
Then down from the sky came the wooden shoe,
  Bringing the fishermen home ;
'T was all so pretty a sail, it seemed
  As if it could not be ;
And some folk thought 't was a dream they 'd
        dreamed
  Of sailing that beautiful sea ;
  But I shall name you the fishermen three :
            Wynken,
            Blynken,
            And Nod.

Wynken and Blynken are two little eyes,
  And Nod is a little head,
And the wooden shoe that sailed the skies
  Is a wee one's trundle-bed ;

So shut your eyes while Mother sings
    Of wonderful sights that be,
And you shall see the beautiful things
    As you rock on the misty sea
    Where the old shoe rocked the fishermen three, —
            Wynken,
            Blynken,
            And Nod.

HUGO'S "FLOWER TO BUTTERFLY."

SWEET, bide with me and let my love
　　Be an enduring tether;
Oh, wanton not from spot to spot,
　　But let us dwell together.

You 've come each morn to sip the sweets
　　With which you found me dripping,
Yet never knew it was not dew
　　But tears that you were sipping.

You gambol over honey meads
　　Where siren bees are humming;
But mine the fate to watch and wait
　　For my beloved's coming.

The sunshine that delights you now
　　Shall fade to darkness gloomy;
You should not fear if, biding here,
　　You nestled closer to me.

So rest you, love, and be my love,
    That my enraptured blooming
May fill your sight with tender light,
    Your wings with sweet perfuming.

Or, if you will not bide with me
    Upon this quiet heather,
Oh, give me wing, thou beauteous thing,
    That we may soar together.

A PROPER TREWE IDYLL OF CAMELOT.

WHENAS ye plaisaunt Aperille shoures have
washed and purged awaye
Ye poysons and ye rheums of earth to make a
merrie May,
Ye shraddy boscage of ye woods ben full of birds
that syng
Right merrilie a madrigal unto ye waking spring,
Ye whiles that when ye face of earth ben washed
and wiped ycleane
Her peeping posies blink and stare like they had
ben her een;
Then, wit ye well, ye harte of man ben turned to
thoughts of love,
And, tho' it ben a lyon erst, it now ben like a
dove!
And many a goodly damosel in innocence beguiles
Her owne trewe love with sweet discourse and
divers plaisaunt wiles.
In soche a time ye noblesse liege that ben Kyng
Arthure hight

Let cry a joust and tournament for evereche errant
      knyght,
And, lo ! from distant Joyous-garde and eche adja-
      cent spot
A company of noblesse lords fared unto Camelot,
Wherein were mighty feastings and passing merrie
      cheere,
And eke a deale of dismal dole, as you shall quickly
      heare.

It so befell upon a daye when jousts ben had and
      while
Sir Launcelot did ramp around ye ring in gallaunt
      style,
There came an horseman shriking sore and rashing
      wildly home, —
A mediæval horseman with ye usual flecks of
      foame;
And he did brast into ye ring, wherein his horse did
      drop,
Upon ye which ye rider did with like abruptness
      stop,
And with fatigue and fearfulness continued in a
      swound
Ye space of half an hour or more before a leech
      was founde.

"Now tell me straight," quod Launcelot, "what
     varlet knyght you be,
Ere that I chine you with my sworde and cleave
     your harte in three!"
Then rolled that knyght his bloudy een, and an-
     swered with a groane, —
"By worthy God that hath me made and shope ye
     sun and mone,
There fareth hence an evil thing whose like ben
     never seene,
And tho' he sayeth nony worde, he bodethe ill, I
     ween.
So take your parting, evereche one, and gird you
     for ye fraye, —
By all that's pure, ye Divell sure doth trend his
     path this way!"
Ye which he quoth and fell again into a deadly
     swound,
And on that spot, perchance (God wot), his bones
     mought yet be founde.

Then evereche knight girt on his sworde and shield
     and hied him straight
To meet ye straunger sarasen hard by ye city
     gate;

Full sorely moaned ye damoseis and tore their beau-
 tyse haire
For that they feared an hippogriff wolde come to
 eate them there ;
But as they moaned and swounded there too numer-
 ous to relate,
Kyng Arthure and Sir Launcelot stode at ye city
 gate,
And at eche side and round about stode many a
 noblesse knyght
With helm and speare and sworde and shield and
 mickle valor dight.

Anon there came a straunger, but not a gyaunt grim,
Nor yet a draggon, — but a person gangling, long,
 and slim ;
Yclad he was in guise that ill-beseemed those knygtly
 days,
And there ben nony etiquette in his uplandish ways ;
His raiment was of dusty gray, and perched above
 his lugs
There ben the very latest style of blacke and shiny
 pluggs ;
His nose ben like a vulture beake, his blie ben swart
 of hue,

And curly ben ye whiskers through ye which ye
    zephyrs blewe;

Of all ye een that ben yseene in countries far or nigh,

None nonywhere colde hold compare unto that
    straunger's eye;

It was an eye of soche a kind as never ben on
    sleepe,

Nor did it gleam with kindly beame, nor did not
    use to weepe;

But soche an eye ye widdow hath, — an hongrey eye
    and wan,

That spyeth for an oder chaunce whereby she may
    catch on;

An eye that winketh of itself, and sayeth by that
    winke

Ye which a maiden sholde not knowe nor never even
    thinke;

Which winke ben more exceeding swift nor human
    thought ben thunk,

And leaveth doubting if so be that winke ben really
    wunke;

And soch an eye ye catte-fysshe hath when that he
    ben on dead

And boyled a goodly time and served with capers
    on his head;

A rayless eye, a bead-like eye, whose famisht aspect
    shows
It hungereth for ye verdant banks whereon ye wild
    time grows ;
An eye that hawketh up and down for evereche kind
    of game,
And, when he doth espy ye which, he tumbleth to
    ye same.

Now when he kenned Sir Launcelot in armor clad,
    he quod,
" Another put-a-nickel-in-and-see-me-work, be
    god ! "
But when that he was ware a man ben standing in
    that suit,
Ye straunger threw up both his hands, and asked
    him not to shoote.

Then spake Kyng Arthure : " If soe be you mind to
    do no ill,
Come, enter into Camelot, and eat and drink your
    fill ;
But say me first what you are hight, and what
    mought be your quest.

Ye straunger quod, " I 'm five feet ten, and fare me
   from ye West ! "
" Sir Fivefeetten," Kyng Arthure said, " I bid you
   welcome here ;
So make you merrie as you list with plaisaunt wine
   and cheere ;
This very night shall be a feast soche like ben never
   seene,
And you shall be ye honored guest of Arthure and
   his queene.
Now take him, good sir Maligraunce, and entertain
   him well
Until soche time as he becomes our guest, as I you
   tell."

That night Kyng Arthure's table round with mighty
   care ben spread,
Ye oder knyghts sate all about, and Arthure at ye
   heade :
Oh,'t was a goodly spectacle to ken that noblesse liege
Dispensing hospitality from his commanding siege !
Ye pheasant and ye meate of boare, ye haunch of
   velvet doe,
Ye canvass hamme he them did serve, and many
   good things moe.

Until at last Kyng Arthure cried: "Let bring my
    wassail cup,
And let ye sound of joy go round, — I 'm going to
    set 'em up !
I 've pipes of Malmsey, May-wine, sack, metheglon,
    mead, and sherry,
Canary, Malvoisie, and Port, swete Muscadelle and
    perry ;
Rochelle, Osey, and Romenay, Tyre, Rhenish, pos-
    set too,
With kags and pails of foaming ales of brown Octo-
    ber brew.
To wine and beer and other cheere I pray you now
    despatch ye,
And for ensample, wit ye well, sweet sirs, I 'm look-
    ing at ye ! "

Unto which toast of their liege lord ye oders in ye
    party
Did lout them low in humble wise and bid ye same
    drink hearty.
So then ben merrisome discourse and passing
    plaisaunt cheere,
And Arthure's tales of hippogriffs ben mervaillous
    to heare ;

But stranger far than any tale told of those knyghts
    of old

Ben those facetious narratives ye Western straunger
    told.

He told them of a country many leagues beyond ye
    sea

Where evereche forraine nuisance but ye Chinese
    man ben free,

And whiles he span his monstrous yarns, ye ladies
    of ye court

Did deem ye listening thereunto to be right plais-
    aunt sport;

And whiles they listened, often he did squeeze a
    lily hande, —

Ye which proceeding ne'er before ben done in
    Arthure's lande;

And often wank a sidelong wink with either roving
    eye,

Whereat ye ladies laughen so that they had like to
    die.

But of ye damosels that sat around Kyng Arthure's
    table

He liked not her that sometime ben ron over by ye
    cable,

Ye which full evil hap had harmed and marked her
    person so
That in a passing wittie jest he dubbeth her ye crow.

But all ye oders of ye girls did please him passing
    well
And they did own him for to be a proper seeming
    swell ;
And in especial Gurnevere esteemed him wondrous
    faire,
Which had made Arthure and his friend, Sir
    Launcelot, to sware
But that they both ben so far gone with posset,
    wine, and beer,
They colde not see ye carrying-on, nor neither
    colde not heare ;
For of eche liquor Arthure quafft, and so did all
    ye rest,
Save only and excepting that smooth straunger
    from the West.
When as these oders drank a toast, he let them
    have their fun
With divers godless mixings, but *he* stock to
    willow run,

Ye which (and all that reade these words sholde
    profit by ye warning)
Doth never make ye head to feel like it ben
    swelled next morning.
Now, wit ye well, it so befell that when the night
    grew dim,
Ye Kyng was carried from ye hall with a howl-
    ing jag on him,
Whiles Launcelot and all ye rest that to his
    highness toadied
Withdrew them from ye banquet hall and sought
    their couches loaded.

Now, lithe and listen, lordings all, whiles I do
    call it shame
That, making cheer with wine and beer, men do
    abuse ye same;
Though eche be well enow alone, ye mixing of
    ye two
Ben soche a piece of foolishness as only ejiots do.
Ye wine is plaisaunt bibbing whenas ye gentles dine,
And beer will do if one hath not ye wherewithal
    for wine,
But in ye drinking of ye same ye wise are never
    floored

By taking what ye tipplers call too big a jag on
    board.

Right hejeous is it for to see soche dronkonness
    of wine

Whereby some men are use to make themselves
    to be like swine;

And sorely it repenteth them, for when they wake
    next day

Ye fearful paynes they suffer ben soche as none
    mought say,

And soche ye brenning in ye throat and brasting
    of ye head

And soche ye taste within ye mouth like one
    had been on dead, —

Soche be ye foul condicions that these unhappy
    men

Sware they will never drink no drop of nony
    drinke again.

Yet all so frail and vain a thing and weak
    withal is man

That he goeth on an oder tear whenever that he
    can.

And like ye evil quatern or ye hills that skirt
    ye skies,

Ye jag is reproductive and jags on jags arise.

Whenas Aurora from ye east in dewy splendor
hied

King Arthure dreemed he saw a snaix and ben
on fire inside,

And waking from this hejeous dreeme he sate
him up in bed, —

"What, ho! an absynthe cocktail, knave! and
make it strong!" he said;

Then, looking down beside him, lo! his lady was
not there —

He called, he searched, but, Goddis wounds! he
found her nonywhere;

And whiles he searched, Sir Maligraunce rashed
in, wood wroth, and cried,

"Methinketh that ye straunger knyght hath snuck
away my bride!

And whiles *he* spake a motley score of other
knyghts brast in

And filled ye royall chamber with a mickle fear-
full din,

For evereche one had lost his wiffe nor colde
not spye ye same,

Nor colde not spye ye straunger knyght, Sir
Fivefeetten of name.

10

Oh, then and there was grevious lamentacion all
    arounde,

For nony dame nor damosel in Camelot ben
    found, —

Gone, like ye forest leaves that speed afore ye
    autumn wind.

Of all ye ladies of that court not one ben left
    behind

Save only that same damosel ye straunger called
    ye crow,

And she allowed with moche regret she ben too
    lame to go;

And when that she had wept full sore, to Arthure
    she confess'd

That Guernevere had left this word for Arthure
    and ye rest:

"Tell them," she quod, "we shall return to them
    whenas we 've made

This little deal we have with ye Chicago Bourde
    of Trade."

BÉRANGER'S "MA VOCATION."

MISERY is my lot,
    Poverty and pain;
Ill was I begot,
    Ill must I remain;
Yet the wretched days
    One sweet comfort bring,
When God whispering says,
    "Sing, O singer, sing!"

Chariots rumble by,
    Splashing me with mud;
Insolence see I
    Fawn to royal blood;
Solace have I then
    From each galling sting
In that voice again, —
    "Sing, O singer, sing!"

Cowardly at heart,
  I am forced to play
A degraded part
  For its paltry pay;
Freedom is a prize
  For no starving thing;
Yet that small voice cries,
  "Sing, O singer, sing!"

I *was* young, but now,
  When I 'm old and gray,
Love — I know not how
  Or why — hath sped away;
Still, in winter days
  As in hours of spring,
Still a whisper says,
  "Sing, O singer, sing!"

Ah, too well I know
  Song 's my only friend!
Patiently I 'll go
  Singing to the end;
Comrades, to your wine!
  Let your glasses ring!
Lo, that voice divine
  Whispers, "Sing, oh, sing!"

CHILD AND MOTHER.

O MOTHER–MY–LOVE, if you 'll give me
    your hand,
  And go where I ask you to wander,
I will lead you away to a beautiful land, —
  The Dreamland that 's waiting out yonder.
We 'll walk in a sweet posie-garden out there,
  Where moonlight and starlight are streaming,
And the flowers and the birds are filling the air
  With the fragrance and music of dreaming.

There 'll be no little tired-out boy to undress,
  No questions or cares to perplex you,
There 'll be no little bruises or bumps to caress,
  Nor patching of stockings to vex you;
For I 'll rock you away on a silver-dew stream
  And sing you asleep when you 're weary,
And no one shall know of our beautiful dream
  But you and your own little dearie.

And when I am tired I 'll nestle my head
   In the bosom that 's soothed me so often,
And the wide-awake stars shall sing, in my stead,
   A song which our dreaming shall soften.
So, Mother-my-Love, let me take your dear hand,
   And away through the starlight we 'll wander, —
Away through the mist to the beautiful land, —
   The Dreamland that 's waiting out yonder.

THE CONVERSAZZHYONY.

WHAT conversazzhyonies wuz I really did not
  know,
For that, you must remember, wuz a powerful spell
  ago ;
The camp wuz new 'nd noisy, 'nd only modrit sized,
So fashionable sossiety wuz hardly crystallized.
There had n't been no grand events to interest the
  men,
But a lynchin', or a inquest, or a jackpot now an'
  then.

The wimmin-folks wuz mighty scarce, for wimmin',
  ez a rool,
Don't go to Colorado much, excep' for teachin'
  school,
An' bein' scarce an' chipper and pretty (like as not),
The bachelors perpose, 'nd air accepted on the
  spot.

Now Sorry Tom wuz owner uv the Gosh-all-Hem-
　　lock mine,
The wich allowed his better haff to dress all-fired
　　fine ;
For Sorry Tom wuz mighty proud uv her, an' she
　　uv him,
Though *she* wuz short an' tacky, an' *he* wuz tall an'
　　slim,
An' *she* wuz edjicated, an' Sorry Tom wuz *not,*
Yet, for *her* sake, he 'd whack up every cussid cent
　　he 'd got !
Waal, jest by way uv celebratin' matrimonial joys,
She thought she 'd give a conversazzhyony to the
　　boys, —
A peert an' likely lady, 'nd ez full uv 'cute idees
'Nd uv etiquettish notions ez a fyste is full uv
　　fleas.

Three-fingered Hoover kind uv kicked, an' said
　　they might be durned
So fur ez any conversazzhyony wuz concerned ;
He 'd come to Red Hoss Mountain to tunnel for
　　the ore,
An' *not* to go to parties, — quite another kind uv
　　bore !

But, bein' he wuz candidate for marshal uv the
 camp,
I rayther had the upper holts in arguin' with the
 scamp ;
Sez I, " Three-fingered Hoover, can't ye see it is
 yer game
To go for all the votes ye kin an' collar uv the
 same ? "
The wich perceivin', Hoover sez, " Waal, ef I *must,*
 I *must ;*
So I 'll frequent that conversazzhyony, ef I
 bust ! "

Three-fingered Hoover wuz a trump ! Ez fine a
 man wuz he
Ez ever caused an inquest or blossomed on a
 tree ! —
A big, broad man, whose face bespoke a honest
 heart within, —
With a bunch uv yaller whiskers appertainin' to
 his chin,
'Nd a fierce mustache turnt up so fur that both his
 ears wuz hid,
Like the picture that you always see in the " Life
 uv Cap'n Kidd."

His hair wuz long an' wavy an' fine ez Southdown
    fleece, —

Oh, it shone an' smelt like Eden when he slicked
    it down with grease!

I 'll bet there wuz n't anywhere a man, all round, ez
    fine

Ez wuz Three-fingered Hoover in the spring uv '69!

The conversazzhyony wuz a notable affair,

The bong tong deckolett 'nd en regaly bein' there;

The ranch where Sorry Tom hung out wuz fitted
    up immense, —

The Denver papers called it a "palashal resi-
    dence."

There wuz mountain pines an' fern an' flowers
    a-hangin' on the walls,

An' cheers an' hoss-hair sofies wuz a-settin' in the
    halls ;

An' there wuz heaps uv pictures uv folks that lived
    down East,

Sech ez poets an' perfessers, an' last, but not the
    least,

Wuz a chromo uv old Fremont, — we liked that
    best, you bet,

For there 's lots uv us old miners that is votin' for
    him yet !

When Sorry Tom received the gang perlitely at the
  door,
He said that keerds would be allowed upon the
  second floor ;
And then he asked us would we like a drop uv ody
  vee.
Connivin' at his meanin', we responded promptly,
  " Wee."
A conversazzhyony is a thing where people
  speak
The langwidge in the which they air partickulerly
  weak :
" I see," sez Sorry Tom, "you grasp what that 'ere
  lingo means."
" You bet yer boots," sez Hoover ; " I 've lived at
  Noo Orleens,
An', though I aint no Frenchie, nor kin unto the
  same,
I kin parly voo, an' git there, too, like Eli, toot lee
  mame ! "

As speakin' French wuz not my forte, — not even
  oovry poo, —
I stuck to keerds ez played by them ez did not
  parly voo,

An' bein' how that poker wuz my most perficient
    game,
I poneyed up for 20 blues an' set into the same.
Three-fingered Hoover stayed behind an' parly-
    vood so well
That all the kramy delly krame allowed he wuz
    the belle.
The other candidate for marshal did n't have a
    show;
For, while Three-fingered Hoover parlyed, ez they
    said, tray bow,
Bill Goslin did n't know enough uv French to git
    along,
'Nd I reckon that he had what folks might call a
    movy tong.

From Denver they had freighted up a real pianny-
    fort
Uv the warty-leg and pearl-around-the-keys-an'-
    kivver sort,
An', later in the evenin', Perfesser Vere de Blaw
Performed on that pianny, with considerble eclaw,
Sech high-toned opry airs ez one is apt to hear,
    you know,
When he rounds up down to Denver at a Emmy
    Abbitt show;

An' Barber Jim (a talented but ornery galoot)
Discoursed a obligatter, conny mory, on the floot,
'Til we, ez sot upstairs indulgin' in a quiet game,
Conveyed to Barber Jim our wish to compromise
      the same.

The maynoo that wuz spread that night wuz mighty
      hard to beat, —
Though somewhat awkward to pernounce, it wuz
      not so to eat:
There wuz puddins, pies, an' sandwidges, an' forty
      kinds uv sass,
An' floatin' Irelands, custards, tarts, an' patty dee
      foy grass;
An' millions uv cove oysters wuz a-settin' round in
      pans,
'Nd other native fruits an' things that grow out
      West in cans.
But I wuz all kufflummuxed when Hoover said
      he'd choose
" Oon peety morso, see voo play, de la cette Char-
      lotte Rooze ; "
I 'd knowed Three-fingered Hoover for fifteen years
      or more,
'Nd I 'd never heern him speak so light uv wimmin
      folks before !

Bill Goslin heern him say it, 'nd uv course *he*
     spread the news

Uv how Three-fingered Hoover had insulted Char-
     lotte Rooze

At the conversazzhyony down at Sorry Tom's that
     night,

An' when they asked me, I allowed that Bill for
     once wuz right;

Although it broke my heart to see my friend go
     up the fluke,

We all opined his treatment uv the girl deserved
     rebuke.

It warnt no use for Sorry Tom to nail it for a
     lie, —

When it come to sassin' wimmin, there wuz blood
     in every eye;

The boom for Charlotte Rooze swep' on an' took
     the polls by storm,

An' so Three-fingered Hoover fell a martyr to
     reform !

Three-fingered Hoover said it wuz a terrible mis-
     take,

An' when the votes wuz in, he cried ez if his heart
     would break.

We never knew who Charlotte wuz, but Goslin's
  brother Dick
Allowed she wuz the teacher from the camp on
  Roarin' Crick,
That had come to pass some foreign tongue with
  them uv our alite
Ez wuz at the high-toned party down at Sorry
  Tom's that night.
We let it drop — this matter uv the lady — there
  an' then,
An' we never heerd, nor wanted to, of Charlotte
  Rooze again,
An' the Colorado wimmin-folks, ez like ez not,
  don't know
How we vindicated all their sex a twenty year
  ago.

For in these wondrous twenty years has come a
  mighty change,
An' most uv them old pioneers have gone acrosst
  the range,
Way out into the silver land beyond the peaks uv
  snow, —
The land uv rest an' sunshine, where all good
  miners go.

I reckon that they love to look. from out the silver
  haze,
Upon that God's own country where they spent
  sech happy days;
Upon the noble cities that have risen since they
  went;
Upon the camps an' ranches that are prosperous
  an' content;
An', best uv all, upon those hills that reach into
  the air,
Ez if to clasp the loved ones that are waitin' over
  there.

PROF. VERE DE BLAW.

ACHIEVIN' sech distinction with his moddel
  tabble dote
Ez to make his Red Hoss Mountain restauraw a
  place uv note,
Our old friend Casey innovated somewhat round
  the place,
In hopes he would ameliorate the sufferins uv the
  race;
'Nd uv the many features Casey managed to im-
  port
The most important wuz a Steenway gran' piannyfort,
An' bein' there wuz nobody could play upon the
  same,
He telegraffed to Denver, 'nd a real perfesser
  came, —

11

The last an' crownin' glory uv the Casey res-
tauraw
Wuz that tenderfoot musicianer, Perfesser Vere de
Blaw !

His hair wuz long an' dishybill, an' he had a yaller
skin,
An' the absence uv a collar made his neck look
powerful thin :
A sorry man he wuz to see, az mebby you'd sur-
mise,
But the fire uv inspiration wuz a-blazin' in his
eyes !
His name wuz Blanc, wich same is Blaw (for that's
what Casey said,
An' Casey passed the French ez well ez any
Frenchie bred);
But no one ever reckoned that it really wuz his
name,
An' no one ever asked him how or why or whence
he came, —
Your ancient history is a thing the Coloradan
hates,
An' no one asks another what his name wuz in the
States !

At evenin', when the work wuz done, an' the miners
    rounded up
At Casey's, to indulge in keerds or linger with the
    cup,
Or dally with the tabble dote in all its native
    glory,
Perfesser Vere de Blaw discoursed his music reper-
    tory
Upon the Steenway gran' piannyfort, the wich wuz
    sot
In the hallway near the kitchen (a warm but quiet
    spot),
An' when De Blaw's environments induced the
    proper pride, —
Wich gen'rally wuz whiskey straight, with seltzer
    on the side, —
He throwed his soulful bein' into opry airs 'nd
    things
Wich bounded to the ceilin' like he 'd mesmerized
    the strings.

Oh, you that live in cities where the gran' piannies
    grow,
An' primy donnies round up, it 's little that you
    know

Uv the hungerin' an' the yearnin' wich us miners
   an' the rest
Feel for the songs we used to hear before we
   moved out West.
Yes, memory is a pleasant thing, but it weakens
   mighty quick;
It kind uv dries an' withers, like the windin' mountain crick,
That, beautiful, an' singin' songs, goes dancin' to
   the plains,
So long ez it is fed by snows an' watered by the
   rains;
But, uv that grace uv luvin' rains 'nd mountain
   snows bereft,
Its bleachin' rocks, like dummy ghosts, is all its
   memory left.

The toons wich the perfesser would perform with
   sech eclaw
Would melt the toughest mountain gentleman I
   ever saw, —
Sech touchin' opry music ez the Trovytory
   sort,
The sollum " Mizer Reery," an' the thrillin' " Keely
   Mort;"

Or, sometimes, from "Lee Grond Dooshess" a
    trifle he would play,
Or morsoze from a opry boof, to drive dull care
    away;
Or, feelin' kind uv serious, he 'd discourse some-
    what in C, —
The wich he called a opus (whatever that may
    be);
But the toons that fetched the likker from the
    critics in the crowd
Wuz *not* the high-toned ones, Perfesser Vere de
    Blaw allowed.

'T wuz "Dearest May," an' "Bonnie Doon," an'
    the ballard uv "Ben Bolt,"
Ez wuz regarded by all odds ez Vere de Blaw's
    best holt;
Then there wuz "Darlin' Nellie Gray," an' "Settin'
    on the Stile,"
An' "Seein' Nellie Home," an' "Nancy Lee," 'nd
    "Annie Lisle,"
An' "Silver Threads among the Gold," an' "The
    Gal that Winked at Me,"
An' "Gentle Annie," "Nancy Till," an' "The Cot
    beside the Sea."

Your opry airs is good enough for them ez likes
    to pay
Their money for the truck ez can't be got no other
    way;
But opry to a miner is a thin an' holler thing, —
The music that he pines for is the songs he used
    to sing.

One evenin' down at Casey's De Blaw wuz at his
    best,
With four-fingers uv old Willer-run concealed be-
    neath his vest;
The boys wuz settin' all around, discussin' folks
    an' things,
'Nd I had drawed the necessary keerds to fill on
    kings;
Three-fingered Hoover kind uv leaned acrosst the
    bar to say
If Casey 'd liquidate right off, *he 'd* liquidate next
    day;
A sperrit uv contentment wuz a-broodin' all around
(Onlike the other sperrits wich in restauraws
    abound),
When, suddenly, we heerd from yonder kitchen-
    entry rise

A toon each ornery galoot appeared to recognize.
Perfesser Vere de Blaw for once eschewed his
    opry ways,
An' the remnants uv his mind went back to earlier,
    happier days,
An' grappled like an' wrassled with a old familiar
    air
The wich we all uv us had heern, ez you have,
    everywhere !
Stock still we stopped, — some in their talk uv
    politics an' things,
I in my unobtrusive attempt to fill on kings,
'Nd Hoover leanin' on the bar, an' Casey at the
    till, —
We all stopped short an' held our breaths (ez a
    feller sometimes will),
An' sot there more like bumps on logs than healthy,
    husky men,
Ez the memories uv that old, old toon come sneakin'
    back again.

You've guessed it ? No, you have n't; for it wuz n't
    that there song
Uv the home we'd been away from an' had hank-
    ered for so long, —

No, sir ; it wuz n't " Home, Sweet Home," though
    it 's always heard around
Sech neighborhoods in wich the home that *is* "sweet
    home " is found.
And, ez for me, I seemed to see the past come back
    again,
And hear the deep-drawed sigh my sister Lucy ut-
    tered when
Her mother asked her if she 'd practised her two
    hours that day,
Wich, if she had n't, she must go an' do it right
    away !
The homestead in the States 'nd all its memories
    seemed to come
A-floatin' round about me with that magic lumty-
    tum.

And then uprose a stranger wich had struck the
    camp that night ;
His eyes wuz sot an' fireless, 'nd his face wuz spook-
    ish white,
'Nd he sez : " Oh, how I suffer there is nobody kin
    say,
Onless, like me, he 's wrenched himself from home
    an' friends away

To seek surcease from sorrer in a fur, seclooded
    spot,
Only to find — alars, too late ! — the wich surcease
    is not !
Only to find that there air things that, somehow,
    seem to live
For nothin' in the world but jest the misery they
    give !
I 've travelled eighteen hundred miles, but that toon
    has got here first ;
I 'm done, — I 'm blowed, — I welcome death, an'
    bid it do its worst ! "

Then, like a man whose mind wuz sot on yieldin'
    to his fate,
He waltzed up to the counter an' demanded whis-
    key straight,
Wich havin' got outside uv, — both the likker and
    the door, —
We never seen that stranger in the bloom uv health
    no more !
But some months later, what the birds had left uv
    him wuz found
Associated with a tree, some distance from the
    ground ;

And Husky Sam, the coroner, that set upon him,
    said
That two things wuz apparent, namely : first, de-
    ceast wuz dead ;
And, second, previously had got involved beyond
    all hope
In a knotty complication with a yard or two uv
    rope !

MEDIÆVAL EVENTIDE SONG.

COME hither, lyttel childe, and lie upon my
    breast to-night,
For yonder fares an angell yclad in raimaunt
    white,
And yonder sings ye angell as onely angells may,
And his songe ben of a garden that bloometh
    farre awaye.

To them that have no lyttel childe Godde some-
    times sendeth down
A lyttel childe that ben a lyttel lambkyn of his owne;
And if so bee they love that childe, He willeth it
    to staye,
But elsewise, in His mercie He taketh it awaye.

And sometimes, though they love it, Godde yearn-
    eth for ye childe,
And sendeth angells singing, whereby it ben be-
    guiled;

They fold their arms about ye lamb that croodleth
    at his play,
And beare him to ye garden that bloometh farre
    awaye.

I wolde not lose ye lyttel lamb that Godde hath
    lent to me;
If I colde sing that angell songe, how joysome I
    sholde bee!
For, with mine arms about him, and my musick in
    his eare,
What angell songe of paradize soever sholde I
    feare?

Soe come, my lyttel childe, and lie upon my breast
    to-night,
For yonder fares an angell yclad in raimaunt white,
And yonder sings that angell, as onely angells may,
And his songe ben of a garden that bloometh farre
    awaye.

MARTHY'S YOUNKIT.

THE mountain brook sung lonesomelike, and
    loitered on its way
Ez if it waited for a child to jine it in its play;
The wild-flowers uv the hillside bent down their
    heads to hear
The music uv the little feet that had somehow
    grown so dear;
The magpies, like winged shadders, wuz a-flutterin'
    to an' fro
Among the rocks an' holler stumps in the ragged
    gulch below;
The pines an' hemlocks tosst their boughs (like
    they wuz arms) and made
Soft, sollum music on the slope where he had
    often played;
But for these lonesome, sollum voices on the moun-
    tain-side,
There wuz no sound the summer day that Marthy's
    younkit died.

We called him Marthy's younkit, for Marthy wuz
the name

Uv her ez wuz his mar, the wife uv Sorry Tom,—
the same

Ez taught the school-house on the hill, way back
in '69,

When she marr'd Sorry Tom, wich owned the
Gosh-all-Hemlock mine !

And Marthy's younkit wuz their first, wich, bein'
how it meant

The first on Red Hoss Mountain, wuz truly a
event !

The miners sawed off short on work ez soon ez
they got word

That Dock Devine allowed to Casey what had
just occurred ;

We loaded up an' whooped around until we all
wuz hoarse

Salutin' the arrival, wich weighed ten pounds, uv
course !

Three years, and sech a pretty child !—his mother's
counterpart !

Three years, and sech a holt ez he had got on every
heart !—

A peert an' likely little tyke with hair ez red ez
    gold,
A laughin', toddlin' everywhere, — 'nd only three
    years old !
Up yonder, sometimes, to the store, an' sometimes
    down the hill
He kited (boys is boys, you know, — you could n't
    keep him still !)
An' there he 'd play beside the brook where purpul
    wild-flowers grew,
An' the mountain pines an' hemlocks a kindly shad-
    der threw,
An' sung soft, sollum toons to him, while in the
    gulch below
The magpies, like strange sperrits, went flutterin'
    to an' fro.

Three years, an' then the fever come, — it wuz n't
    right, you know,
With all us old ones in the camp, for that little
    child to go ;
It 's right the old should die, but that a harmless
    little child
Should miss the joy uv life an' love, — that can't
    be reconciled !

That's what we thought that summer day, an' that
    is what we said
Ez we looked upon the piteous face uv Marthy's
    younkit dead.
But for his mother's sobbin', the house wuz very
    still,
An' Sorry Tom wuz lookin', through the winder,
    down the hill,
To the patch beneath the hemlocks where his dar-
    lin' used to play,
An' the mountain brook sung lonesomelike an'
    loitered on its way.

A preacher come from Roarin' Crick to comfort
    'em an' pray,
'Nd all the camp wuz present at the obsequies
    next day;
A female teacher staged it twenty miles to sing a
    hymn,
An' we jined her in the chorus, — big, husky men
    an' grim
Sung "Jesus, Lover uv my Soul," an' then the
    preacher prayed,
An' preacht a sermon on the death uv that fair
    blossom laid

Among them other flowers he loved, — wich ser-
    mon set sech weight
On sinners bein' always heeled against the future
    state,
That, though it had been fashionable to swear a
    perfec' streak,
There warnt no swearin' in the camp for pretty
    nigh a week !

Last thing uv all, four strappin' men took up the
    little load
An' bore it tenderly along the windin', rocky
    road,
To where the coroner had dug a grave beside the
    brook,
In sight uv Marthy's winder, where the same could
    set an' look
An' wonder if his cradle in that green patch, long
    an' wide,
Wuz ez soothin' ez the cradle that wuz empty at
    her side ;
An' wonder if the mournful songs the pines wuz
    singin' then
Wuz ez tender ez the lullabies she'd never sing
    again,

'Nd if the bosom uv the earth in wich he lay at
    rest
Wuz half ez lovin' 'nd ez warm ez wuz his mother's
    breast.

The camp is gone; but Red Hoss Mountain rears
    its kindly head,
An' looks down, sort uv tenderly, upon its cher-
    ished dead;
'Nd I reckon that, through all the years, that little
    boy wich died
Sleeps sweetly an' contentedly upon the mountain-
    side;
That the wild-flowers uv the summer-time bend
    down their heads to hear
The footfall uv a little friend they know not slum-
    bers near;
That the magpies on the sollum rocks strange
    flutterin' shadders make,
An' the pines an' hemlocks wonder that the sleeper
    does n't wake;
That the mountain brook sings lonesomelike an'
    loiters on its way
Ez if it waited for a child to jine it in its play.

IN FLANDERS.

THROUGH sleet and fogs to the saline bogs
 Where the herring fish meanders,
An army sped, and then, 't is said,
 Swore terribly in Flanders:

  "—— —— —— ——!"
  "—— —— —— ——!"

A hideous store of oaths they swore,
 Did the army over in Flanders!

At this distant day we 're unable to say
 What so aroused their danders;
But it 's doubtless the case, to their lasting disgrace,
 That the army swore in Flanders:

  "—— —— —— ——!"
  "—— —— —— ——!"

And many more such oaths they swore,
 Did that impious horde in Flanders!

Some folks contend that these oaths without end
  Began among the commanders,
That, taking this cue, the subordinates, too,
  Swore terribly in Flanders:
        'T was "—— —— ——!"
        "—— —— —— ——!"

Why, the air was blue with the hullaballoo
  Of those wicked men in Flanders!

But some suppose that the trouble arose
  With a certain Corporal Sanders,
Who sought to abuse the wooden shoes
  That the natives wore in Flanders.
        Saying: "—— —— ——!"
        "—— —— —— ——!"

What marvel then, that the other men
  Felt encouraged to swear in Flanders!

At any rate, as I grieve to state,
  Since these soldiers vented their danders
Conjectures obtain that for language profane
  There is no such place as Flanders.
        "—— —— —— ——!"
        "—— —— —— ——!"

This is the kind of talk you 'll find
  If ever you go to Flanders.

How wretched is he, wherever he be,
   That unto this habit panders!
And how glad am I that my interests lie
   In Chicago, and not in Flanders!

        "____. ____ ____ ____!"
        "____. ____ ____ ____!"

Would never go down in this circumspect town
   However it might in Flanders.

OUR BIGGEST FISH.

WHEN in the halcyon days of eld, I was a
    little tyke,
I used to fish in pickerel ponds for minnows and
    the like;
And oh, the bitter sadness with which my soul
    was fraught
When I rambled home at nightfall with the puny
    string I 'd caught!
And, oh, the indignation and the valor I 'd display
When I claimed that all the biggest fish I 'd caught
    had got away!

Sometimes it was the rusty hooks, sometimes the
    fragile lines,
And many times the treacherous reeds would foil
    my just designs;
But whether hooks or lines or reeds were actually
    to blame
I kept right on at losing all the monsters just the
    same —

I never lost a *little* fish — yes, I am free to say
It always was the *biggest* fish I caught that got
away.

And so it was, when later on, I felt ambition
pass
From callow minnow joys to nobler greed for pike
and bass ;
I found it quite convenient, when the beauties
would n't bite
And I returned all bootless from the watery chase
at night,
To feign a cheery aspect and recount in accents
gay
How the biggest fish that I had caught had somehow got away.

And really, fish look bigger than they are before
they 're caught —
When the pole is bent into a bow and the slender
line is taut,
When a fellow feels his heart rise up like a dough-
nut in his throat
And he lunges in a frenzy up and down the leaky
boat !

Oh, you who 've been a-fishing will indorse me
    when I say
That it always *is* the biggest fish you catch that
    gets away!

'T is even so in other things — yes, in our greedy
    eyes
The biggest boon is some elusive, never-captured
    prize;
We angle for the honors and the sweets of human
    life —
Like fishermen we brave the seas that roll in end-
    less strife;
And then at last, when all is done and we are spent
    and gray,
We own the biggest fish we've caught are those
    that got away.

I would not have it otherwise; 'tis better there
    should be
Much bigger fish than I have caught a-swimming
    in the sea;
For now some worthier one than I may angle for
    that game —

May by his arts entice, entrap, and comprehend
    the same;
Which, having done, perchance he'll bless the man
    who's proud to say
That the biggest fish he ever caught were those
    that got away.

THIRTY-NINE.

O HAPLESS day! O wretched day!
　I hoped you 'd pass me by —
Alas, the years have sneaked away
　And all is changed but I!
Had I the power, I would remand
　You to a gloom condign,
But here you 've crept upon me and
　I — I am thirty-nine!

Now, were I thirty-five, I could
　Assume a flippant guise;
Or, were I forty years, I should
　Undoubtedly look wise;
For forty years are said to bring
　Sedateness superfine;
But thirty-nine don't mean a thing —
　A bas with thirty-nine!

You healthy, hulking girls and boys, —
  What makes you grow so fast?
Oh, I 'll survive your lusty noise —
  I 'm tough and bound to last!
No, no — I 'm old and withered too —
  I feel my powers decline,
(Yet none believes this can be true
  Of one at thirty-nine).

And you, dear girl with velvet eyes,
  I wonder what you mean
Through all our keen anxieties
  By keeping sweet sixteen.
With your dear love to warm my heart,
  Wretch were I to repine;
I was but jesting at the start —
  I 'm glad I 'm thirty-nine!

So, little children, roar and race
  As blithely as you can,
And, sweetheart, let your tender grace
  Exalt the Day and Man;
For then these factors (I 'll engage)
  All subtly shall combine
To make both juvenile and sage
  The one who 's thirty-nine!

Yes, after all, I 'm free to say
   I would much rather be
Standing as I do stand to-day,
   'Twixt devil and deep sea;
For though my face be dark with care
   Or with a grimace shine,
Each haply falls unto my share,
   For I am thirty-nine!

'T is passing meet to make good cheer
   And lord it like a king,
Since only once we catch the year
   That does n't mean a thing.
O happy day! O gracious day!
   I pledge thee in this wine —
Come, let us journey on our way
   A year, good Thirty-Nine!

Sept. 2, 1889.

YVYTOT.

WHERE wail the waters in their flow
A spectre wanders to and fro,
And evermore that ghostly shore
Bemoans the heir of Yvytot.

Sometimes, when, like a fleecy pall,
The mists upon the waters fall,
Across the main float shadows twain
That do not heed the spectre's call.

The king his son of Yvytot
Stood once and saw the waters go
Boiling around with hissing sound
The sullen phantom rocks below.

And suddenly he saw a face
Lift from that black and seething place—
Lift up and gaze in mute amaze
And tenderly a little space,

A mighty cry of love made he —
No answering word to him gave she,
   But looked, and then sunk back again
Into the dark and depthless sea.

And ever afterward that face,
That he beheld such little space,
   Like wraith would rise within his eyes
And in his heart find biding place.

So oft from castle hall he crept
Where mid the rocks grim shadows slept,
   And where the mist·reached down and kissed
The waters as they wailed and wept.

The king it was of Yvytot
That vaunted, many years ago,
   There was no coast his valiant host
Had not subdued with spear and bow.

For once to him the sea-king cried:
" In safety all thy ships shall ride
   An thou but swear thy princely heir
Shall take my daughter to his bride.

"And lo, these winds that rove the sea
Unto our pact shall witness be,
　And of the oath which binds us both
Shall be the judge 'twixt me and thee!"

Then swore the king of Yvytot
Unto the sea-king years ago,
　And with great cheer for many a year
His ships went harrying to and fro.

Unto this mighty king his throne
Was born a prince, and one alone —
　Fairer than he in form and blee
And knightly grace was never known.

But once he saw a maiden face
Lift from a haunted ocean place —
　Lift up and gaze in mute amaze
And tenderly a little space.

Wroth was the king of Yvytot,
For that his son would never go
　Sailing the sea, but liefer be
Where wailed the waters in their flow,

The winds went riding to and fro
And scourged the waves that crouched below,
   And bade them sing to a childless king
The bridal song of Yvytot.

So fell the curse upon that shore,
And hopeless wailing evermore
   Was the righteous dole of the craven soul
That heeded not what oath he swore.

An hundred ships went down that day
All off the coast of Norroway,
   And the ruthless sea made mighty glee
Over the spoil that drifting lay.

The winds went calling far and wide
To the dead that tossed in the mocking tide;
   "Come forth, ye slaves! from your fleeting grave
And drink a health to your prince his bride!"

Where wail the waters in their flow
A spectre wanders to and fro,
   But nevermore that ghostly shore
Shall claim the heir of Yvytot.

Sometimes, when, like a fleecy pall,
The mists upon the waters fall,
  Across the main flit shadows twain
That do not heed the spectre's call.

LONG AGO.

I ONCE knew all the birds that came
    And nested in our orchard trees;
For every flower I had a name —
    My friends were woodchucks, toads, and bees;
I knew where thrived in yonder glen
    What plants would soothe a stone-bruised toe —
Oh, I was very learned then;
    But that was very long ago!

I knew the spot upon the hill
    Where checkerberries could be found,
I knew the rushes near the mill
    Where pickerel lay that weighed a pound!
I knew the wood, — the very tree
    Where lived the poaching, saucy crow,
And all the woods and crows knew me —
    But that was very long ago.

And pining for the joys of youth,
    I tread the old familiar spot
Only to learn this solemn truth:
    I have forgotten, am forgot.
Yet here's this youngster at my knee
    Knows all the things I used to know;
To think I once was wise as he —
    But that was very long ago.

I know it's folly to complain
    Of whatsoe'er the Fates decree;
Yet were not wishes all in vain,
    I tell you what my wish should be:
I'd wish to be a boy again,
    Back with the friends I used to know;
For I was, oh! so happy then —
    But that was very long ago!

TO A SOUBRETTE.

'T IS years, soubrette, since last we met;
      And yet — ah, yet, how swift and tender
My thoughts go back in time's dull track
      To you, sweet pink of female gender !
I shall not say — though others may —
      That time all human joy enhances ;
But the same old thrill comes to me still
      With memories of your songs and dances.

Soubrettish ways these latter days
      Invite my praise, but never get it ;
I still am true to yours and you —
      My record 's made, I 'll not upset it !
The pranks they play, the things they say —
      I 'd blush to put the like on paper,
And I 'll avow they don't know how
      To dance, so awkwardly they caper !

I used to sit down in the pit
   And see you flit like elf or fairy
Across the stage, and I 'll engage
   No moonbeam sprite were half so airy;
Lo, everywhere about me there
   Were rivals reeking with pomatum,
And if, perchance, they caught your glance
   In song or dance, how did I hate 'em!

At half-past ten came rapture — then
   Of all those men was I most happy,
For bottled beer and royal cheer
   And tête-à-têtes were on the tapis.
Do you forget, my fair soubrette,
   Those suppers at the Café Rector, —
The cosey nook where we partook
   Of sweeter cheer than fabled nectar?

Oh, happy days, when youth's wild ways
   Knew every phase of harmless folly!
Oh, blissful nights, whose fierce delights
   Defied gaunt-featured Melancholy!
Gone are they all beyond recall,
   And I — a shade, a mere reflection —
Am forced to feed my spirits' greed
   Upon the husks of retrospection!

And lo! to-night, the phantom light,
   That, as a sprite, flits on the fender,
Reveals a face whose girlish grace
   Brings back the feeling, warm and tender;
And, all the while, the old-time smile
   Plays on my visage, grim and wrinkled, —
As though, soubrette, your footfalls yet
   Upon my rusty heart-strings tinkled!

SOME TIME.

LAST night, my darling, as you slept,
　　I thought I heard you sigh,
And to your little crib I crept,
　　And watched a space thereby;
And then I stooped and kissed your brow,
　　For oh! I love you so—
You are too young to know it now,
　　But some time you shall know!

Some time when, in a darkened place
　　Where others come to weep,
Your eyes shall look upon a face
　　Calm in eternal sleep,
The voiceless lips, the wrinkled brow,
　　The patient smile shall show—
You are too young to know it now,
　　But some time you may know!

Look backward, then, into the years,
    And see me here to-night —
See, O my darling ! how my tears
    Are falling as I write;
And feel once more upon your brow
    The kiss of long ago —
You are too young to know it now,
    But some time you shall know.

THE END.